NOTHING BUT THE NIGHT

JOHN BLACKBURN was born in 1923 in the village of Corbridge, England, the second son of a clergyman. Blackburn started attending Haileybury College near London in 1937, but his education was interrupted by the onset of World War II; the shadow of the war, and that of Nazi Germany, would later play a role in many of his works. He served as a radio officer during the war in the Mercantile Marine from 1942 to 1945, and resumed his education afterwards at Durham University, earning his bachelor's degree in 1949. Blackburn taught for several years after that, first in London and then in Berlin, and married Joan Mary Clift in 1950. Returning to London in 1952, he took over the management of Red Lion Books.

It was there that Blackburn began writing, and the immediate success in 1958 of his first novel, *A Scent of New-Mown Hay*, led him to take up a career as a writer full-time. He and his wife also maintained an antiquarian bookstore, a secondary career that would inform some of Blackburn's later work. A prolific author, Blackburn would write nearly 30 novels between 1958 and 1985; most of these were horror and thrillers, but also included one historical novel set in Roman times, *The Flame and the Wind* (1967). He died in 1993.

GREG GBUR is an associate professor of physics and optical science at the University of North Carolina at Charlotte. He writes the long-running blog "Skulls in the Stars," which discusses classic horror fiction, physics and the history of science, as well as the curious intersections between the three topics. His science writing has recently been featured in "The Best Science Writing Online 2012," published by Scientific American. He has previous introduced John Blackburn's *Broken Boy* and *Bury Him Darkly* for Valancourt Books.

By John Blackburn

*A Scent of New-Mown Hay**

A Sour Apple Tree

*Broken Boy**

Dead Man Running

The Gaunt Woman

*Blue Octavo**

Colonel Bogus

The Winds of Midnight

A Ring of Roses

Children of the Night

*The Flame and the Wind**

*Nothing but the Night**

The Young Man from Lima

*Bury Him Darkly**

Blow the House Down

*The Household Traitors**

Devil Daddy

For Fear of Little Men

Deep Among the Dead Men

*Our Lady of Pain**

Mister Brown's Bodies

*The Face of the Lion**

*The Cyclops Goblet**

Dead Man's Handle

The Sins of the Father

*A Beastly Business**

The Book of the Dead

*The Bad Penny**

* Available or forthcoming from Valancourt Books

NOTHING BUT THE NIGHT

by

JOHN BLACKBURN

Oh never fear, man, nought's to dread,
Look not left nor right:
In all the endless road you tread
There's nothing but the night.
A. E. HOUSMAN: A Shropshire Lad

With a new introduction by
GREG GBUR

𝕶𝖆𝖓𝖘𝖆𝖘 𝕮𝖎𝖙𝖞:
VALANCOURT BOOKS
2013

Nothing but the Night by John Blackburn
First published London: Jonathan Cape, 1968
First Valancourt Books edition 2013

Copyright © 1968 by John Blackburn
Introduction © 2013 by Greg Gbur

Published by Valancourt Books, Kansas City, Missouri
Publisher & Editor: JAMES D. JENKINS
20th Century Series Editor: SIMON STERN, University of Toronto
http://www.valancourtbooks.com

Library of Congress Cataloging-in-Publication Data

Blackburn, John, 1923-
Nothing but the night / by John Blackburn ;
with a new introduction by Greg Gbur.
pages cm. – (20th Century Series)
ISBN 978-1-939140-24-1 *(acid-free paper)*
1. Murder–Investigation–England–Fiction. 2. Mystery fiction. I. Title.
PR6052.L34N68 2013
823'.914–dc23
2013007048

All Valancourt Books publications are printed on acid free paper
that meets all ANSI standards for archival quality paper.

Design and typography by James D. Jenkins
Set in Dante MT 11/13.5

10 9 8 7 6 5 4 3 2 1

INTRODUCTION

JOHN BLACKBURN's twelfth book *Nothing but the Night* highlights a unique "what if?" scenario for the works of the master horror author. It is the only Blackburn novel to have been adapted into a major motion picture,[1] a 1973 movie of the same name starring the iconic actors Christopher Lee and Peter Cushing. The movie did poorly at the box office, evidently ending prospects, at least in the short term, of further adaptations. If it had been a hit, however, John Blackburn's work, with its fast-paced plots, surprising twists and turns, and surprise endings, could have easily kept the movie industry in business for quite some time. *Nothing but the Night*, one of Blackburn's most macabre works, should have been the perfect beginning to a long movie run.

English-born John Fenwick Blackburn (1923-1993) certainly provided enough material to form the basis for a successful string of films. Incredibly prolific, he wrote 28 novels between *A Scent of New-Mown Hay* in 1958 and *The Bad Penny* in 1985, on average roughly one book per year. His writing career started while he was working as the director of Red Lion Books in London; when his first book became successful, he resigned in order to write full-time, though he managed an antiquarian bookstore with his wife Joan Clift. Even before writing, Blackburn's life and career took nearly as many twists as one of his typical novels: he worked at various times as a schoolteacher (in both London and Berlin), a lorry driver, and a radio officer in the Mercantile Marine during World War II.

Blackburn's writing lies at a nearly unique intersection of the genres of horror, mystery and thriller. All of his books are fast-paced, filled with unexpected perils, narrow escapes, and sudden twists that send the story in a different direction. Nearly all of his books also provide a mystery of some sort, which is explained

---

1 There was, however, also a made-for-television movie in 1969 titled *Destiny of a Spy*, based on Blackburn's novel *The Gaunt Woman*.

with an unexpected revelation in its climax. However, as often as not that revelation turns out involve a particularly nasty, even supernatural, horror. Part of the joy in reading a Blackburn novel without any foreknowledge is the surprise of seeing exactly what kind of threat is driving the plot.

Like many thrillers, *Nothing but the Night* begins with a small event: in this case, the crash of a school bus carrying children from the Van Traylen Home, an orphanage on the isolated Isle of Bala off the northwest coast of Scotland. The driver dies of his injuries, but the children are fine – except for young Mary Valley, whose injuries are psychological and inexplicable. The girl seems to be suffering from flashbacks or hallucinations of a traumatic and devastating fire, an event that she could not have experienced herself. Mr Haynes, the attending psychiatrist, goes against the wishes of the Van Traylen Fellowship and holds Mary for further evaluation, going so far as to bring a hospital colleague, the respected bacteriologist Sir Marcus Levin, into his confidence.

Convinced that Mary is in a dangerous mental state, Haynes decides on a risky course of action: he brings Mary's biological mother, Anna Harb, for a family reunion. Harb is troubled herself, having originally lost her daughter while spending time in prison for a triple homicide. She is also convinced that she has psychic powers, and in a first meeting with Haynes declares that her daughter is in fact dead. The meeting of mother and daughter does not go well, culminating with Anna attempting to throw Mary down a flight of stairs, screaming that the young girl is a fiend from hell. Mary is rescued, but Anna escapes. When it is discovered that Anna has murdered again, a nationwide manhunt is initiated.

This macabre set of circumstances draws the attention of General Charles Kirk, member of Her Majesty's Foreign Intelligence Service. Kirk has already been investigating the Van Traylen Fellowship, a collection of some thirty wealthy benefactors funding good works throughout the country, including the Van Traylen Home. Over a very short period of time, a handful of Fellowship members have met seemingly accidental but suspicious deaths, including its founder, Helen Van Traylen. Is someone trying to eliminate the Fellowship, and is the attempt on Mary Valley's life somehow connected? Marcus Levin and General Kirk join forces to get to the bottom of the mystery.

When Anna Harb's car is found abandoned on the ferry to the Isle of Bala, the location of the Van Traylen Home, an island-wide search begins for the murderess. But many more surprises, and incredible horror, lie in wait for Kirk and Levin on the island – culminating in the darkness of Guy Fawkes night.

As noted above, Blackburn is a master of surprise twists in his storytelling. *Nothing but the Night* is a somewhat unusual novel in that, to borrow some boxing parlance, Blackburn telegraphs his blow quite early in the story. Most readers will determine almost right away that there is something sinister about the seemingly innocent young girl Mary Valley. However, to continue the boxing analogy, when the blow finally does strike home and the true secret is revealed, the reader will likely find that it hits much harder than expected.

Evil children had in fact become a popular horror theme at the time that Blackburn wrote *Nothing but the Night*. The most influential of such stories is certainly John Wyndham's 1958 novel *The Midwich Cuckoos*, in which the women of the small town of Midwich become mysteriously impregnated with babies that grow into children of supernatural powers and extraterrestrial origin. This novel was made into a 1960 movie titled *Village of the Damned*, which was successful enough to spawn a sequel in 1963, *Children of the Damned*. Other stories of the era that featured evil children include William March's 1954 novel *The Bad Seed*, about a murderous sociopathic young girl, Ira Levin's 1967 novel *Rosemary's Baby*, introducing the child of Satan, and Jerome Bixby's 1953 short story *It's a Good Life*, about a young boy with godlike powers who terrorizes and dominates his fellow townsfolk. All of these had successful television or movie adaptations, indicating how compelling the idea had become.

It is unclear, however, exactly why children became not only acceptable as monstrous villains but also popular as such. March's *The Bad Seed*, mentioned above, suggests one possibility. By the early 1900s, the public had become quite aware of the scientific debate of "nature versus nurture": are one's personality traits inherited biologically from one's parents (nature) or do they come from environmental factors including parenting (nurture)? Anthropological work by Margaret Mead on the island of Samoa in the 1920s suggested nurture was extremely important, but a growing understanding of genetic inheritance seemed to weigh in favor of nature. *The Bad Seed* falls directly on the nature side, suggesting that its young heroine, Rhoda, acquired her murderous tendencies from her grandmother. *The Midwich Cuckoos* also features children who are predestined to be dangerous, in this case thanks to alien manipulation. Stories such as these capitalize on a parent's natural fears.

The movie version of *The Bad Seed*, released in 1956, suggests another reason why bad children could serve as good horror fodder. The end of the film concludes with a theatrical curtain call, and culminates with Patty McCormack (Rhoda) being spanked by actress Nancy Kelly (playing her mother). This rather bizarre light-hearted scene intends to reassure parents that, in spite of what the movie might have shown them, a good bit of parenting could have prevented everything! Parenting itself was going through dramatic changes thanks to the 1946 publication of *Baby and Child Care* by Dr. Benjamin Spock. Spock's book, which was second in sales only to the Bible in its first 52 years, suggested treating children as individuals and adjusting parenting to be less punitive and more based on understanding. To its critics, *Baby and Child Care* encouraged permissiveness, leading to selfishness and instant gratification in children. It is not too far of a leap to imagine such undisciplined children becoming monsters. Books such as *Nothing but the Night* could therefore be said to indulge in parenting fears.

Nothing but the Night's use of an evil child is also illustrative of how John Blackburn was willing to tap into whatever horror ideas were captivating readers at the time. Another example is his 1959 novel *Broken Boy* (also published by Valancourt), whose story of a sinister demonic cult seems inspired by the stories of Satanism and witchcraft by fellow Englishman Dennis Wheatley such as *The Devil Rides Out* (1934). Also noteworthy is Blackburn's 1976 novel *The Face of the Lion*, which presents a remarkably ahead of its time threat of a zombie holocaust, possibly inspired by George Romero's 1968

landmark film *Night of the Living Dead.* Though Blackburn might
have drawn inspiration from other works, it is important to note
that he is never derivative: each of his novels stands on its own and
takes the initial concept to a uniquely horrifying destination.

Blackburn is known for the use of recurring stock characters in
his novels. *Nothing but the Night* brings back three of them: General
Charles Kirk, Doctor Marcus Levin, and journalist John Forest.
General Kirk is a high-ranking member of the Foreign Intelligence
Service, and applies powerful detective skills and a blunt pragma-
tism to the investigation. Doctor Levin, a researcher in bacteria
and a recent Nobel Prize winner, has the scientific know-how to
unravel the complicated forces at play on the Isle of Bala. John
Forest is portrayed as a ruthless and cynical man who will do any-
thing for a story, and tends to cause as many problems as he solves.
By *Nothing but the Night*, Kirk and Levin have worked on a number
of cases together, including Blackburn's first two novels *A Scent of
New-Mown Hay* and *A Sour Apple Tree.*

The use of such characters has often been presented as a nega-
tive in Blackburn's work; however, they almost become old friends
after one has read through enough of his novels. Later books will
bring different groups together to solve a problem, and I've found
an odd thrill in discovering that two favorites will team up in a
newly acquired book.

Though Blackburn's books often feel ahead of their time in
terms of pacing and ideas, they still contain antiquated concepts
that nevertheless give insight into the history of his time. Early
in *Nothing but the Night*, General Kirk tries to solve the mystery
of the Van Traylen murders by feeding all known information
about the case into a semi-intelligent computer; the computer
then returns a print-out confirming that the data suggests a conspiracy against the Fellowship! This view of computing power was
obviously over-optimistic: to this day, the closest we have come to
such open-ended intelligence is Deep Blue's win in chess over Gary
Kasparov in 1997 and the 2011 win of IBM's Watson over past "Jeop-
ardy!" champs such as Ken Jennings. Over-hyping of the power of
computers was relatively common at that time, however. The television show *The Prisoner* included an episode titled "The General"

which first aired on November 3, 1967; this episode also featured a brilliant computer which could answer almost any question posed it, given enough data. The titular prisoner, Number 6, defeats the machine by asking it the unanswerable question: "Why?"

Even a super-intelligent computer could not have foreseen the fate of the movie version of *Nothing but the Night*, which seemed to have everything going for it. Riding a wave of popularity for gruesome stories of black magic, Christopher Lee set up his own production company – Charlemagne – to produce Blackburn's tale and, as noted earlier, starred in it himself along with his good friend and other veteran horror actor Peter Cushing. The failure of the movie led immediately to Charlemagne's demise, though Lee himself did not blame the source material. In his autobiography,[1] he notes that *Nothing but the Night* "failed because it was ahead of its time."

This may be true; watching the movie today, however, my impression is that it really failed for more mundane reasons. Though the screenplay is remarkably loyal to the plot of the novel, the tone and pacing feel poorly handled. Whereas Blackburn's novel feels like an ever-accelerating chain of events leading inexorably to disaster, the movie scenes seem leisurely and disconnected. Blackburn's book draws the reader along, while the movie feels like a collection of isolated incidents. Though the casting of Lee as Colonel Charles Bingham (replacing General Kirk) and Cushing as Sir Mark Ashley (replacing Marcus Levin) is inspired, other key roles seem poorly handled. Evidently John Blackburn himself was disappointed[2] with the casting of actress Diana Dors as Anna Harb, and she does come across as more comical than threatening with fiery red hair and a bright red jacket. In the book, Anna Harb is unseen after arriving on the Isle, making her a figure of menace. In the movie, we are treated to numerous scenes of Harb stumbling across the landscape, hiding from the police search parties. Nevertheless, the movie maintains the horrifying finale of the book, and is fascinating to watch.

1 Christopher Lee, *Lord of Misrule* (London: Orion Books Ltd, 2003), p. 227.
2 Stated in the trivia section of the Internet Movie Database entry for *Nothing but the Night*.

In any case, the book *Nothing but the Night* was well-received by critics, as were the majority of Blackburn's novels. The most noteworthy review was written by Francis Iles in the November 15, 1968 issue of *The Guardian* newspaper. Iles wrote, "John Blackburn lives right up to his reputation for the eerie and the sinister in Nothing but the Night (Cape, 21s); a little girl has nightmares, but were they nightmares? Indeed, was she only a little girl?"

Hopefully this new edition will draw attention back to the long and unfairly neglected works of John Blackburn. Though the first attempt to convert his work to cinema failed, his writing seems a natural, almost inevitable, fit to the big screen.

GREG GBUR
March 5, 2013

Nothing but the Night

Preface

FOUR PEOPLE found Helen Van Traylen and three of them were close friends. Lord Michael Fawnlee had known her since she was a girl, Dr Eric Yeats was her medical adviser and had attended her during her several illnesses, while Jane Vince had been her house-keeper and companion for over twenty years. The exception was a Church of England curate named Glossop, who knew of Mrs Van Traylen's charitable activities and had called to collect a subscription for Oxfam.

Fawnlee and Yeats had been talking to Glossop when they heard the explosion and, being elderly, it took them some time to mount the stairs, while the clergyman did not presume to push past them. On the landing they met Jane Vince and Mary Valley, a small child from the Van Traylen Home who had been staying with her bene-factress during the past fortnight. They were both in tears and Miss Vince could only point dumbly towards the door of the bedroom. Yeats was the first to enter the room and he and Fawnlee smiled with relief as their eyes grew accustomed to the dim light.

'Thank God, Eric,' Fawnlee said. 'It was just a car backfiring in the street and Jane is getting old like the rest of us. She imagines things and you've been frightening her about Helen's condition.'

The curtains were half drawn and in the dusk they could see their friend stretched peacefully out on a sofa in an attitude they had seen a score of times before. She was dressed in the famil-iar pale-blue housecoat, her walking stick was by her side and an Abyssinian cat named Oscar Wilde was crouched on her shoulder as if guarding his sleeping mistress. Then Jane Vince switched on the lights and screamed.

Not a stick but a small-bore shotgun lay between Mrs Van Tray-len's wrinkled hands and Oscar Fingall O'Flahertie Wills Wilde, to give him his full title, was busily licking the little that was left of her face.

'Eight green bottles hanging on the wall . . . Eight green bottles hanging on the wall.' Almost a year had passed since Helen Van Traylen died and through the open windows of the motor coach 'Surrey Monarch' the children's voices rang shrill and clear above the sounds of the traffic and a church clock starting to strike six.

'And if one green bottle should accidentally fall, there'd be seven green bottles hanging on the wall.' The bus drew up at the Marford Lane traffic lights and two women waiting for their signal to cross the road smiled up at the faces of the little boys and girls sitting in twos and singing so tunefully. Nice kids, they thought. Well dressed and obviously well brought up. Probably some private school on their way back from an outing. Very different from the young hooligans who were dragging down the neighbourhood since those new council flats had been built last year. All singing in tune and all looking so happy.

'Five green bottles hanging on the wall.'

'Noisy little bastards!' Frank Reynolds, the coach driver, muttered to himself as the lights changed and he accelerated across the junction. He felt ill and tired, the rush hour traffic was building up and he was due to deliver the party at London Airport by six thirty sharp.

'And if one green bottle . . .' He had a headache, probably the 'flu coming on, the 'Monarch'—all the company's vehicles bore regal names—needed tuning and this constant singing was no help at all. If only the perishers would change to another song it wouldn't be so bad, but they'd been through their blasted bottles four times already. Why couldn't those old cows who were supposed to be in charge quieten them down? Reynolds glowered at two grey-haired ladies across the aisle, but they were deep in conversation and appeared oblivious of the singing.

No discipline with the youngsters these days. He considered the straps and canes of his own school days. No respect for adults, no consideration for anybody and the little blonde madam at his side was the worst of the lot. Whenever the others came to the end of the chant she turned around and started them off again. Reynolds lit a cigarette to calm his frayed nerves and changed gear for the approaching roundabout at Pounder's Corner. The sky was clear but the road surface was still damp from an afternoon shower and the time was almost three minutes past six.

Exactly a minute later when the forty-ninth bottle was in process of demolition, the 'Surrey Monarch' appeared to go out of control, mounted the pavement and came to rest with its radiator inside the Period Lounge of the Grey Bull public house on the corner of Pounder's Green. The coach was back in service within the month but, apart from structural damage to the Bull, the insurers had to write off a large quantity of imitation Victorian chaise-longues, Georgian carriage lamps, and Tudor weapons. There were only three casualties. The licensee, a certain Major Treacher, was deprived of a toe by a falling halberd and a seven-year-old girl named Mary Valley received superficial cuts and bruises. Frank Reynolds, who had held a clean licence for thirty-five years and worked for his present employers for over eight of them, died in hospital within an hour of the collision.

Chapter One

'YOU are of course aware of the presence of antibodies in the animal system, ladies and gentlemen.' Sir Marcus Levin, K.C.B., F.R.S., and recent winner of a Nobel prize for services to medicine, fingered his already immaculate tie and smiled at the assembled class of students.

'These tiny creatures which live in symbiosis with our cells act as allies; shock troops against the ever-present armies of bacteria and virus infections which constantly threaten us. Without this support it would be quite impossible for the human race to survive.' Marcus paused to glance up at the clock. There was another five minutes left for him to finish his introductory talk and then he would have a quick lunch at his club and hurry round to the Central Research Laboratory. He had been pleased when asked to deliver a series of lectures at Saint Bede's Hospital, but now that his present work looked like paying off he begrudged the time bitterly. Less than three miles away, a tiny creature which could save

the lives of millions was stirring in its plastic saucers and he longed
to be there to observe what happened.

'The dangers of the indiscriminate use of antibiotics are equally
well known to you all.' He gave a winning smile at a pretty girl
in the front row. 'Though these substances can kill some of the
germs which attack us they may also weaken the friendly allies
which are our natural defence against infection. Should another
invasion take place before the organisms have had time to recover,
the human system is left open and helpless against attack.' The
minute hand jerked forward and Marcus started to gather up his
notes as he spoke.

'What present-day research is looking for is a solution to this
problem: a means of changing the very nature of these antibodies,
of producing—I hate the word mutant since it came into popular
use, but it is the only one which fits—a creature that is resistant to
the worst we can do to it and becomes even more inimical to our
enemies. That will be the subject of these lectures, and next week
I shall draw your attention to the work of Edelman in Munich,
Trevor-Jones in New York and a team of bacteriologists here in
London. We are all searching for what may well be the impossible:
a really super defence mechanism against disease. If we succeed,
mankind may die of over-population and starvation, but that is
quite outside my province.' He gave another smile as he closed his
briefcase and the clock moved on to the hour.

'Thank you very much for listening to me, ladies and gentlemen, and I am looking forward to our next meeting.' He bowed to
them and hurried out of the room: a tall, imposing figure but, if
one looked closely at his face, the marks of suffering were visible
beneath the debonair consultant's manner.

'Ah, there you are, Sir Marcus. I've managed to catch you, then.'
A porter intercepted him in the corridor, grinning widely because
they were old friends. 'The dean asked me to give you a message.
Said he wanted to see you on a matter of some urgency.' The man
smiled again as he saw Marcus's expression and he lowered his voice.

'Look, sir, you go on if you're in a hurry, and I'll say I missed
you. Knowing Dr Plunkett, I shouldn't think it's anything which
can't wait.'

'You tempt me, Serjeant. You tempt me very strongly indeed.' They had estimated that the culture would reach its maximum activity at approximately two o'clock and Marcus dearly wanted to be at Central Research to see what happened—if anything. The chances were that this would turn out to be just another failure. All the same, if it did react in the way they hoped, a real breakthrough would have been made. He stood considering for a moment and then shrugged and put on what his wife called 'Your wounded stag expression'.

'No, you are a good friend, but get thee behind me, Serjeant Jackson.' He turned and walked quickly away towards a staircase.

'Come in, Sir Marcus. Jackson managed to catch you then.' Brian Plunkett, dean of the hospital, came from behind his desk and extended a hand. 'Good of you to spare me a few minutes . . . very good indeed.'

Plunkett was an old, stocky Irishman and his grey beard and red-rimmed eyes had earned him the nickname of 'Badger' to generations of students and housemen. He had little concern with actual medicine nowadays and passed his time listening to endless complaints about finance, hospital management and staff protocol.

'Smoke . . . a glass of something . . . an aperitif before your lunch?' The dean panted slightly as if he, not Marcus, had been running up the stairs.

'No, thank you, Doctor.' Marcus shook his head. 'I don't want to appear rude, but I am in a bit of a hurry, so could we get down to business straight away.'

'Of course, of course. You young fellers are always on the go these days.' Plunkett waved him to a chair. Marcus was forty-five years old but he might have been talking to a first-year student. 'I'll be as brief as I can, but as you're on the board of management now this is very much your business. A nasty business too which could be very embarrassing to Saint Bede's. It doesn't do to offend people, you know, Sir Marcus. Not rich and important people like these Van Traylen guardians. You'll have heard of them of course.'

'A little. They are a philanthropic society founded by a Mrs Helen Van Traylen, the widow of an American millionaire. Wasn't she in the news some time ago?'

'About a year ago, Sir Marcus.' The dean started to fill an old charred pipe. 'The poor old bird complained of stomach cramps and Eric Yeats found there was an inoperable tumour. Nothing to look forward to except drugs or extreme pain for the rest of her life, so she blew her head off with a shotgun. Very sad, but the society she started continues to function. The Van Traylen Fellowship, they call it.' The Badger struck a match and clouds of grey smoke drifted across his dingy little office everybody called the 'earth'.

'Rather a moving story in a way. A group of elderly people, all rich, all widowed and childless, who decided to devote their remaining years to good works. They've shelled out thousands on cancer and other medical research, bought a mansion on the west coast of Scotland and turned it into an orphanage, paid a quarter of a million to stop that Warwickshire art collection going abroad. The orphanage is quite a place from all accounts. The kids, there are only about thirty of them, I think, have got their own qualified teachers, a swimming pool, a cinema, and there's even a retired quack living on the premises. No expense spared in fact. When that party were up in London last week, they put them up at Clark's Hotel in Knightsbridge; pots of money. No, that Fellowship is not the kind of organization any sane man would wish to offend.'

'I'm sure you're right, Dean, but how do they concern us?' Marcus looked pointedly at his watch, but Plunkett completely ignored the gesture.

'They concern us very unpleasantly, Sir Marcus, and, if I may say so, you should keep in touch with current affairs. I know how important your work is but it's a narrow vision that can only take in what it sees through a microscope.' The pipe had gone out and he relit it with agonizing slowness.

'If you'd read the papers, you'd know that last Wednesday a party of the Van Traylen children who had spent a week in London sightseeing were involved in an accident. The coach taking them to the airport and a plane back to Scotland went out of control and crashed into a public house somewhere near Hounslow. Mercifully there were only three casualties: the publican, a bogus major called Treacher who had a toe sliced clean off by an imitation halberd, the driver who was crushed by the steering-wheel and died shortly after being admitted here and a seven-year-old girl. Have a look at young Taylor's report on her.'

'If I must.' Marcus glanced briefly at the house surgeon's notes. 'A cut on the cheek and the right shoulder, neither of which required stitching, bruises on both thighs, some signs of slight shock. I don't understand, Dean. This child was in no danger and I presume she has been discharged by now.'

'Yes, any sane man would presume that, Sir Marcus. Any competent physician would have had that child out of here days ago.' Plunkett stood up and paced angrily across the room. 'But not our tame head shrinker; not your friend Mr Peter Haynes, B.M., Dip. Psych., and all the rest of it. Because of the shock, Taylor, quite properly, asked Haynes to look at the child and he came up with this load of gibberish.' The dean opened a filing cabinet and pulled out a bundle of foolscap, which he carried back to the desk as though it were an extremely disgusting object.

'After a brief examination of the little girl, her name is Mary Valley, Haynes stated that she was not suffering from shock but from some obscure mental illness which might be dangerous. He goes on about nervous lesions, a breakdown of the self-regarding sentiment and schizophrenic tendencies. Utter rubbish. Neither you nor I have any training in psychiatry, but we do know that schizophrenia is a physical illness and unrecognizable before puberty. Read it for yourself.'

'Thank you.' Marcus frowned over the first sheet of spidery writing. Plunkett was right in saying that he and Peter Haynes were friends, but he cursed the man for not typing his notes and using a flood of technical jargon which was largely meaningless to him.

'This is beyond me, Dean. But what is the driver's statement Haynes keeps referring to? I thought the man died shortly after being admitted here.'

'Oh that.' The Badger growled and his little pink eyes glowered at the manuscript. 'The man died, but he talked, raved rather, before he lost consciousness. He kept repeating that the child, Mary Valley, was responsible for the accident. Said she had snatched his cigarette and stabbed him in the cheek with it. Complete non-sense, because eight witnesses, two of them adults, stated that the girl was sitting perfectly peacefully beside him right up to the time that the coach went out of control. The police are quite satisfied that the accident was caused by his taking a roundabout too fast, and it is clear to me that the poor fellow was delirious when he made his statement. He'd held a clean licence for thirty-five years and obviously wanted a scapegoat to justify himself.'

'But all the same you decided to back Haynes up, Dean.' Marcus had come to the end of the report and saw Plunkett's neat recommendation attached to the last page.

'That I did, Sir Marcus. I don't like the feller and I don't trust him. Though he's well under forty, Mr Haynes has got through three wrecked marriages and held almost a dozen appointments before coming to us. The board would never have taken him on if it hadn't been for the staff shortage.

'All the same, I make a point of backing up my staff and I tele-phoned Lord Fawnlee, who has been chairman of the Fellowship since Mrs Van Traylen died, and told him that we wanted to keep Mary here for further examination.'

'What was his reaction?' Marcus looked at his watch again. If only Plunkett would come to the point, he thought. He'd have to do without lunch, but there was still time for him to get to Central Research. Success or another failure; a useless product which had cost him six months' work or a tiny creature that might save mil-lions of lives? His colleagues would be on their way there already, eagerly anticipating the moment when a drop of green liquid would spread across a slide and tell them if half a year had not been in vain.

'His lordship threw the book at me good and proper, Sir Marcus.' The dean's old, barking voice broke into his thoughts. 'He said that the child was completely normal and happy and if she had recov-ered from her physical injuries she must be released at once and taken back to join the other children in Scotland. He pointed out that the orphanage had a fully qualified medical officer of its own and finished by saying that one of his employees would be here to collect her by nine o'clock this morning.

'He was quite within his rights of course. Unless the little girl were suffering from some infectious disease that could make her a danger to others, we have no right to hold her against the wish of her parents or legal guardians. A law which I entirely disagree with, Sir Marcus, but there is nothing we can do about it.

'I told Haynes that and it's clear to me that he's the one who needs medical attention. He kept demanding that we apply to a magistrate for a withholding order. Said that the child was in a critical state of mental health and that he couldn't answer for her sanity if she was removed from his care. He finished by giving me a lecture on Jungian archetypes which I have always considered an unscientific attempt to prove human immortality. The fellow will have to go, Levin.' The Badger tugged at his beard to emphasize the decision. 'He may be a pal of yours, but I won't keep an unbalanced man like Haynes on the staff any longer than I have to.'

'You said he was excited, unbalanced about the case?' Marcus frowned slightly. 'Strange that, because I had lunch with Peter only yesterday and showed him round my lab afterwards. We were over three hours together and, though he talked a lot of his own shop, he never mentioned Mary Valley once.

'So that's why you called me up here, Dean. Haynes's contract expires next month and you don't want to renew it. You think that, because I'm friendly with him, I may oppose you on the board.' He pushed back his chair and stood up.

'I shan't fight you, Dr Plunkett, but I think you're making a mistake. You are a physician and I am a bacteriologist and we know little about psychiatry. Though Haynes may appear eccentric I believe him to be a good doctor, and perhaps Mary Valley is mentally ill. In any event she will have left the hospital by now and be on her way to Scotland, so the case is closed as far as Saint Bede's is concerned.'

'Sir Marcus, you really surprise me.' Plunkett broke in with a long, slow shake of the head. 'You believe that I have been wasting your and my own time to discuss Haynes's blasted contract! Mary Valley is not on her way to Scotland. She is still here, in this building, and it was as a bacteriologist that I wished to consult you.' He turned and walked towards the door, his dragging feet showing the trace of a slight Parkinson's syndrome.

'That child remains in our care because in the early hours of the morning she really did become ill; physically, dangerously ill. A nurse heard her crying and went into her room. The pulse rate was ninety-two, the temperature a hundred and six and she was sweating heavily. Later she broke out in a rash on the chest and abdomen. I wanted to give you a general picture of the situation before you examine her. That is why I have been keeping you here.'

He shook his head again as he saw Marcus's expression. 'No, we have not been talking while a little girl is dying, Sir Marcus. Mary is completely out of danger but the hospital is not. Lord Fawnlee has already accused us of crass negligence, and at the moment I am unable to refute him.' Plunkett pulled open the door and prepared to lead the way down the corridor.

'Something came very near to killing that child this morning and I am hoping you will be able to tell me what it was.'

They had put Mary Valley in a private room at the back of 'B' isolation ward and a young nurse opened the door and stepped out into the corridor.

'She is better, gentlemen, very much better,' she said. 'On Mr Haynes's instructions I gave her another adult shot of Genomycin at noon and now the temperature is well under a hundred and the breathing much easier.'

'Mr Haynes told you to administer Genomycin; a full adult dosage?' Marcus raised his eyebrows. The antibiotic was one of the most recently produced, barely out of the experimental stage, and Haynes was not a physician. The man really had taken a good deal on his shoulders.

'I understand it was Mr Haynes who first attended the child, Nurse?'

'Yes, sir. Sister Martin who is on night duty told me that he's been looking in on Mary during the small hours of the morning since she was admitted. He told Sister that he wanted to study the child's sleep patterns. When Sister found that Mary was running a fever she went to call the doctor on duty, but Mr Haynes met her in the corridor and said he would handle the case. I think Sister was rather annoyed about it, sir.'

'I can imagine that, Nurse.' Marcus remembered Sister Martin as a grim martinet who would stand no nonsense from a senior consultant let alone a mere bachelor of medicine. 'But Mr Haynes got his way?'

'Yes, Sir Marcus. But Sister sent for Dr Bryn-Williams and he and Mr Haynes decided to administer Genomycin. It worked almost at once, Sister Martin said. Within an hour the temperature was down and the pulse slower.'

'Did it indeed?' Thank you, Nurse, I'll have a look at her myself now.' Marcus opened the door and stepped into a room which was bright with flowers and gaily painted furniture and Beatrix Potter wallpaper. His frown vanished as he approached the cot by the window and the thin autumn sunshine lit up the smile of his best bedside manner, with its aura of strength and confidence and professional ability. 'Sir Marcus is here and there is nothing to worry about. The danger is past because the specialist has arrived.'

'Hullo, Mary,' he said. 'My name is Dr Levin and I've come to tell you that you're a very good girl and are getting well quickly.' Marcus beamed down at the face on the pillow and Mary Valley smiled back at him. She had strikingly blonde hair and blue eyes which contrasted strangely with a rather dark skin.

'Hullo, Doctor.' The child's voice was sleepy but quite calm and unafraid. 'Are you a proper doctor? Not like Mr Haynes? I heard Sister Martin say that he is only a bachelor of medicine. Have you come to tell me that I can go home?'

'I hope so, Mary. Yes, I think you will be going home very soon.' Marcus studied the faint mottling beneath her chin. Because of that the dean would be within his rights to keep her in hospital. The rash might be contagious, but he had no idea what had caused it. Certainly no common infection like measles or chicken pox, and clearly it was on the decline now. Genomycin might have saved Mary Valley, but he doubted it. The mottling suggested a sweat rash or a nervous allergy. Whatever Peter Haynes had said, the child appeared calm and in excellent mental health, but she had been in a motor accident and shock could produce strange symptoms at times.

'Aren't you happy here, Mary?' Marcus patted the yellow bear on the pillow beside her. 'Don't you and your teddy like being with us?'

'It's all right, Doctor, except when Mr Haynes keeps bothering me, but it's not my home. You should see the home Auntie Van Traylen made for us, Doctor Levin. Right up on an island at the top of Scotland and the house has towers and turrets like a real castle.' The blue eyes gleamed at the memory. 'I have to get back there for the parties. The first one is for Auntie Helen's birthday when all the guardians come to visit us. Matron says that though Auntie is in heaven now, she will be there as well to enjoy the fun.'

'Did she, Mary?' Marcus fought back a frown. Helen Van Traylen had died very horribly by her own hand and this matron sounded a neurotic and unwholesome woman. 'And what is the second party, dear?'

'It's November the fifth, of course, when we burn Guy Fawkes. Didn't you have bonfire parties when you were a little boy, Doctor?'

'We had fires, Mary.' Marcus could almost hear the rattle of machine guns, smell the smoke of the blazing buildings and see tracer bullets arching up over the Warsaw Ghetto.

'Mary . . . Mary Valley,' he said pushing aside the memory as he took her wrist. The child was quite cool and the pulse almost normal, yet the chart on the bedhead told him that her temperature had been up to a hundred and seven. 'That's a pretty name for a very pretty little girl. How old are you, Mary?'

'I am seven years, nine months and three weeks old. But Valley is only one of my names, Doctor.' The child's expression altered slightly and he saw a trace of suspicion in her eyes. 'I used to be called Mary Harb, but Auntie Van Traylen changed it to Valley when I was staying with her a week before she had her accident and went away. She said Valley was much prettier. When are you going to let me go home, Doctor Levin?'

'As soon as I can, Mary, and Mrs Van Traylen was right. It is a much prettier name.' Harb . . . Mary Harb. Where have I heard that name before? Marcus wondered. Not Mary, though. It was Anna Harb that rang a bell, but he couldn't place it.

'Now, let's have a look at your chest, my dear, and we'll soon see it you can go to those parties. Let's hope it's a treasure chest that will buy you a ticket to Scotland.' Marcus reached out to loosen the pyjama jacket, but the child forestalled him, her little fingers working quickly at the buttons while she smiled coyly up at him. Haynes really was an unbalanced fool, he thought. There was no trace of mental abnormality here, though Mary Valley would lead some man quite a dance when she came to maturity.

'So, there they are.' Though his outwardly confident manner remained, Marcus wasn't smiling any more. The rash was light purple and rather beautiful and it curved across the chest like the crescent of a new moon. Certainly an allergy and he felt he knew why it had not been recognized. Mary Valley was out of danger, but if that shot of Genomycin had not been injected in time she might have been disfigured for the rest of her life.

But it is impossible, he thought, taking a lens from his pocket and craning forward. You are jumping to a conclusion without evidence because this is your pet subject. Something else has caused this rash; something similar. You must be mistaken. Not even a maniac would go to such lengths. There was a mist of anger before his eyes and his heart beats quickened as the picture came into focus. The child's chest was covered with five pointed stars and each star was of uniform height and diameter.

Marcus forced his hand steady and he knew that there was no doubt at all. When he had last seen such a rash it was on the shaven skin of an animal, and the organism which caused it was the product of his own laboratory.

Chapter Two

'THEN THE mine-er, forty-nine-er, soon began to peak and pine.' Though Marcus sang in a vain attempt to control anger, his normally tuneful voice was harsh and savage and his knuckles were white on the steering wheel.

'Thought he oughter jine his daughter . . .' The gears grated loudly when the traffic lights changed and he hurled his Ferrari forward with complete disregard for the speed limit. 'Now he's with his Clementine.'

But to hell with Clementine and her bloody father. Kaldorella 6—that was what he should be thinking about. That was the preparation which had entered . . . no, been deliberately introduced into Mary Valley's bloodstream. That was the demon which could have scarred her as badly as the smallpox if Genomycin had not caught it in time. Without that one little-used, unproved antibiotic, the rash would have spread, the pustules increased in size till they opened, became contagious and not only the child but a lot of other people been disfigured for life.

The Kaldorella cultures, named after their discoverer, Professor Feodor Kaldor of Budapest, had been the first attempt to produce a man-made antibody, and though Kaldor had started successfully he had failed disastrously. Somewhere along the line he had gone wrong. His organisms were efficient bactericides, but the vast majority of human beings were allergic to them and their cells revolted, producing the rash and the fever in the battle for survival. Preparation 6 was the most virulent of all Kaldor's products, because not only were the side effects contagious but it appeared resistant to every antibiotic with the exception of Genomycin. Some months ago, Marcus and the four other bacteriologists who made up Central's research team had explored a means to turn this maneater into a friend. They had failed, but cultures had been retained in his lab—the laboratory around which he had shown Peter Haynes only yesterday and where Peter had been left alone for several minutes while he himself was called to the phone. So far, Marcus had not mentioned his suspicions to the dean. He had stated that Mary was out of danger but, though the rash was unlikely to be contagious, she should remain in quarantine till they knew its cause. In a very few minutes he intended to tell Peter that he would personally ruin him.

Greenham Gate. That was where the bastard lived, and for once there was a parking space before the drab block of flats. The tyres scraped the kerb as Marcus shot into it, and he tugged savagely at the handbrake. He had just switched off the ignition when the door was opened for him and a face smiled down from the pavement.

'Mark! You're here at last, dear chap,' said Peter Haynes. 'Almost

two o'clock. I thought you would have discovered my little deception hours ago and been round before lunch.'

'But of course you can break me, Mark. I have no doubts on that
score, old boy. You can throw me out of Saint Bede's, have me
struck off the register, even get me a stretch in prison, I shouldn't
wonder.' Haynes had a sharp Cockney accent and there was mock-
ery in the use of his out-of-date 'old boys' and 'dear chaps'. He was
a thin, wispy man of thirty-seven, with untidy fair hair and thick
glasses. Behind the glasses his eyes looked as if they were out of
focus.

'But will you, that's the point. After all, what have I done?
Certainly I stole a quantity of the Kaldorella culture while your
back was turned yesterday. Yes, I injected some of the stuff into
Mary. But was she in any physical danger? You told me all about
the culture, remember. That an adult dose of Genomycin would
destroy the organism before the rash could cause permanent scars
or become contagious, and I made quite certain that Sister Martin
administered the antibiotic in time and in sufficient quantity. All I
did was to make a little girl feel sick for a few hours, and I have no
regrets at all. I had to gain time, you see. I had to stop her leaving
the hospital till I've finished my examinations.'

'Listen to me, Peter. It's you who are ill, not that little girl. You
must be crazy, completely out of your mind.' Marcus had expected
a denial, then an abject plea, and this bland admission horrified
him. 'We're not in Nazi Germany. We can't use human beings for
medical experiment.'

'I'm not crazy, Mark. Only worried, very worried indeed.'
Haynes leaned wearily back in his chair. The sitting-room-cum-
study of his flat was overflowing with books and papers and
there was obviously no wife or housekeeper to disturb his untidy
comfort.

'You were the first friend I made when I came to Saint Bede's,
but I am not going to appeal to that friendship. At the same time,
I recognize you as an expert in your field and I think you should
do the same for me in mine. That child looks normal to you just
as I might not recognize a person in the early stages of bubonic

plague. But I tell you that Mary Valley is a very sick and dangerous little girl indeed and needs expert treatment. The Van Traylen
people were demanding her release and they were within their
legal rights. I had to find some means of keeping her in the hospital and I have not the slightest regret for what I did.'

'Dangerous? A seven-year-old girl.' Though Marcus was trying
to stop smoking he pulled out a cigarette. He had always regarded
Brian Plunkett as intolerant and out-of-date but the old boy could
be right in describing Haynes and the majority of 'head shrinkers'
as unbalanced.

'Children grow into adults, my dear chap.' Haynes took a lighter
from his desk and held it out for him. 'If Adolf Hitler had received
treatment when he was seven your parents could still be alive and
you might not have rotted in a concentration camp. Besides, several people have suffered from Mary's illness already: she herself,
the publican and the coach driver who had a wife and two children.'

'Yes, I believe the driver's story, Mark.' Haynes kept flicking
the lighter on and off as he brushed aside Marcus's interruption.
'Mary has a morbid fascination towards fire and the very sight of
the man lighting his cigarette could have set it off. I know that as
fact, because I left this lighter by her cot as an experiment. She
played with it quite normally and then, when she thought I wasn't
looking, she held the flame before the face of her teddy bear.'

'All kids do things like that, Peter.' Though Marcus made himself appear unimpressed, he remembered how the child's eyes had
lit up at the thought of the Guy Fawkes Party.

'They don't repeatedly dream about fire and pain, old boy; not
well-balanced children. They don't have one recurrent night terror
and talk in their sleep about men and animals being burned alive.
They don't experience real, physical agony in their sleep. But Mary
Valley does, Mark.' Haynes put down the lighter and started to
rummage through the littered papers on his desk.

'Mary has had that dream each night she has been in our care,
and under mild hypnosis she related it in great detail. She describes
a small room with a metal door and she is locked inside it. The
door is becoming red with heat and beyond it she can hear the bellowing of beasts and a man screaming.' Peter Haynes had found

what he wanted and squinted short-sightedly at a sheet of foolscap.

'I made a tape-recording of that session with her, Mark, which I will play back to you later. What I hope you will notice is the detail she goes into. The room smells of burning rubber; there is a peep hole in the door and a scatter gun hanging on one wall. Another wall contains a safe with a brass plaque displaying its maker's name, the Linksville Corporation, Detroit. Mary talks about the flames spreading across the 'knocking pen' and the 'mutton hoist' falling. As you know I lived for a year in the States, but it took a Dictionary of American Slang to tell me that those terms describe pieces of specialized equipment which are only used in the Middle West canning industry.

'Little Mary Valley knew them though; rather strange that. And why should a seven-year-old child who has never been out of England speak of "scatter" gun instead of shotgun?'

'Perhaps someone told her the story, Peter.' Marcus stood up and crossed over to the window. The earlier promise of a fine day was fading and the sky hinted at rain. By now his colleagues at Central must have finished their tests on the antibody and somehow he knew they would have recorded another failure. 'What's your diagnosis, Peter?'

'I have no definite diagnosis, only a suspicion which I need time to verify. I hope that you will give me that time, Mark. I also hope that my suspicions are completely groundless.' As Marcus turned from the window he could see the hint of a plea behind Haynes's thick lenses.

'If Mary was older I would say she was a schizophrenic, though as we know so little about schizophrenia it's a term I detest. I do believe in what Karl Jung called archetypes, however. Racial and family memories, perhaps from generations back, which have returned and become lodged in the minds of the living.'

'Memories of the dead.' Marcus dragged at his cigarette and frowned. 'I have the greatest respect for Jung as a pioneer, but you're talking more like a witch doctor than a scientist, Peter.'

'Maybe I am, old chap, but ours is a very youthful science.' Haynes was rummaging through his papers again. 'All I know is that Mary is obsessed by something she could not have experienced personally, and the wealth of detail makes it unlikely that she heard the story from a third person. From the little time I have had with Mary I am quite certain the condition will become progressive and incurable unless she has treatment. If I can help that little girl, Mark, I don't give a damn if I have broken my oath, stolen from your laboratory or even risked my liberty.' Haynes craned forward over a photograph he had finally located in the litter on the desk.

'Unless you have me under lock and key, I am meeting Mary's mother soon and I hope she may help to put me a little nearer to the truth.'

'But I thought she was an orphan.' Harb . . . Anna Harb. Once more the name ran through Marcus's memory, but he still could not recall where he had heard it.

'No, about half the Van Traylen children were removed from their parents on account of cruelty or neglect and Mary has a mother all right; rather a celebrated one. Her name is Anna Harb. Surely the dean told you about her visit to Saint Bede's?'

'He never mentioned the woman at all.'

'Really. The old fool sticks to his parrot cry that any publicity is bad publicity where his precious hospital is concerned. But I thought you would have remembered her story, old boy. It made quite a stir at the time.' Haynes was still staring at the photograph as if unable to take his eyes off it.

'Anyway, Anna Harb arrived at the hospital on the morning after Mary was admitted. One of the newspapers had featured the crash and she had seen the child's picture. She demanded to see her daughter and when they refused, became violent and abusive. She shouted that the police and the welfare authorities had kidnapped the girl and now the orphanage people had destroyed her soul. It took Serjeant Jackson and two nurses to get her out of the building.

'I wish I had been there, Mark. If I can only talk to that woman and understand her own illness, I may be able to understand her daughter's. Please give me the time I need, old chap.' He looked up and slid the photograph across the desk. There was a clear plea in Haynes's face now and a nervous tic tugged at the corner of his mouth.

'Give me a chance, Mark. Cover up for a day or two. When you've heard my recording, you'll know that we have to help that little girl.'

'I'll listen to it, Peter, but I'm making no promises.' Marcus was beginning to have the uncomfortable feeling that Haynes's highly unprofessional conduct might possibly be justified. He picked up the photograph and held it to the light, seeing a dark, heavy-faced woman seated against a white background. A trace of coloured blood was clear in the crinkly hair and the thick features, and her eyes stared balefully at the camera as if she were drugged or drunk or under hypnosis.

'That's my patient's mother. That's Mary Valley's heredity.' Haynes nodded as Marcus turned to the newspaper cutting clipped to the margin of the picture. The print was old and faded, but the headlines were clear enough. 'Public Anxiety at Release of Triple Murderess.'

Chapter Three

NINE O'CLOCK and the evening was cold and dank. Mist was rising from the river as the District Line train rattled across a bridge, and the buildings on the opposite bank were barely visible against the sodden sky.

The next station would be his. Peter Haynes glanced at the system map, dropped his cigarette and ground it out with his foot. He felt worried and excited and pleased with himself all at the same time. Worried because Mary Valley's condition was so obviously progressive, excited because it might lead him to a real breakthrough into the causes of certain mental illnesses, pleased with himself because . . . No, that was not really true. He was no longer capable of feeling self-satisfaction because so many of the causes he had followed were clearly lost before he had even joined them. Three marriages and eleven jobs had collapsed because of his fruitless crusading and he would probably lose the battle for Mary's sanity as well. All the same, as far as the practical attempt to help her was concerned, things were not going too badly.

'Very well, Peter.' Marcus Levin had nodded when the tape finally ended and that weeping, whimpering, sometimes screaming voice with its tale of fire and pain had become silent. 'I agree that the child does appear to be in great distress and I'll cover up as you ask. I will state that Mary is suffering from some nervous allergy which I am unable to identify and sign a recommendation that she should remain in quarantine till the rash has cleared up. That should get you a six-day receiving order. Good luck, Peter.'

Marcus had touched his hand briefly and walked out of the flat without another word.

Yes, so far things were going well. The Van Traylen Fellowship had demanded a second opinion, but their man had confirmed Marcus's findings and the order was made. He had another four days and nights to discover the thing which slept in Mary's mind and racked her when it woke. Tonight might give him the first clue to its identity.

But what a short time it was and so far he'd got nowhere. A child who appeared completely normal on the surface but during sleep or under narco-analysis was shown to be very ill indeed. A recurrent dream of fire and bellowing animals and a door growing red. And all described in detail which made it unlikely she was merely repeating a story which she had read or had had repeated to her. Haynes recalled a case reported in Paris before the war. An Indian labourer had been operated on for a brain tumour. The man's family had lived in France for generations and French was known to be his only conscious language. Yet, while under the influence of the anaesthetic he had suddenly begun to rave in fluent Hindi. Could Mary Valley be dreaming of something which had happened to one of her ancestors years ago? Peter Haynes considered himself a humanist, but every minute he had spent with Mary had given him the uncomfortable feeling that it might take a priest rather than a doctor to help her.

Thames Vale. The train drew up at a station which was still in Greater London, but the weeping trees and a border of rhododendrons alongside the platform made it look as if he were in the depths of the country. Only three other passengers alighted— two young women and a grotesquely fat man in an astrakhan coat—and the ticket collector gave Haynes his directions in detail. 'Straight on till you come to the Crown Hotel, then left as far as Saint Mark's Church where you go left again. Saint Mark's, mind, not Saint Mary's, or you'll be in trouble. Carry on from the church till you see Mason's Stores at the next corner, and then branch right to the Bull and Bear public house . . .' Haynes was soon out of his depth in local topography, but he gathered that if he walked in the general direction of the river all would be well.

Yes, it was a foul evening and the night would be worse. Cold and dark with the mist thickening over every suburban garden and clinging around the street lamps like fur. A real Dickensian evening for Bill Sykes or Daniel Quilp to be going about their sinister businesses.

'A wild animal tamed.' That was how Dickens had described Mr Jaggers's housekeeper, and he might be on his way to meet a very similar person: a woman with convictions for larceny, prostitution and assault before she was nineteen and a triple murderess before her twenty-first birthday. All the same she was the one person who might help him to understand Mary's condition and it was an extraordinary piece of luck that he had managed to trace her so quickly thanks to his next-door neighbour, a retired c.i.d. inspector named Milton.

Anna Harb was a mulatto and, as Milton remarked, 'No oil painting even when she was young,' though she made a success of prostitution and supported a ponce named Alfie Bates whom she adored. Alfie, on the other hand, had grown weary of her neurotic moods and rather sinister charms and had deserted her for a Greek hostess in a club called the Blue Heaven in Soho.

A kind friend told her where they could be found and somehow Anna managed to obtain a .32 automatic. Armed with this and fifteen tablets of drinamyl, she went round to the club and pumped lead into Bates and Miss Kypragoros till the pistol was empty. In the course of the action an unfortunate barman received a ricochet through the centre of his forehead and Anna was sent to Broadmoor for life. But ten years later a team of visiting psychiatrists re-examined her case, the Home Secretary was impressed by their findings and she was released.

'You want to talk to her, Mr Haynes?' Milton had said when he questioned him in the saloon bar of their local public house. 'Then just fetch the "E" to "K" telephone directory from the booth and we'll see what we can do.'

'Thanks. My guess is that she'll be listed in here all right.' The inspector had put on his spectacles and started to flip through the book. 'Most killers change their names when they come out, but not Madame Harb who set herself up as a clairvoyant and fortune-teller. Probably a lot of nuts like to have their hands read by a convicted murderess and it's good for business. Yes, here you are, and I will have just one more pint for the road, as you're so kind.'

Larceny, assault, prostitution, murder. The mother of a fair-haired child who had been removed from her care and placed in an orphanage. A little girl who dreamed of fire and tortured animals and who might . . . just might have jabbed a lighted cigarette into the face of a coach driver named Frank Reynolds.

'Penny for the guy. Spare a penny for the guy.' The street had opened up into a dank grassy square and three small boys loomed before him. They had with them a perambulator occupied by a grotesque figure wearing a cardboard mask and an old bowler hat.

'I'll make it a shilling if you can tell me how to get to the Rose and Crown.' Peter Haynes had little sympathy with the burning of the frustrated assassin, but he was completely lost.

'The Rose, guv'?' A grimy hand snatched the coin from his grasp. 'Go right across the Green here, and then turn left at the end towards the river where you'll see the fairground, though it's closed. All shut down for the winter. The pub's just beyond there.'

'Penny for the guy, sir. Spare a penny for the guy.' The stout man he had seen at the station rounded a corner and the boys turned their attention to him.

The fairground was closed all right. It lay on a strip of wasteland at the edge of the river with a faded sign announcing 'Fred Mison's Carnival Attractions', but there was not a light showing from the caravans and roundabouts and boarded-up booths, though one of the roundabouts was not yet covered by a tarpaulin and its horses' heads sneered out at him through the mist. Somewhere downstream a tug bellowed twice and there was a plume of amber flame from the gas-works on the opposite bank. The scene was not so much sinister as sad and depressing, and only one thing relieved the gloom: a brightly lit public house beyond the fair which was his destination.

'Now, sir, what will yours be?' The Irish barman was very young but he handled the drink and change like a veteran. The saloon lounge was only half full and in some other part of the building an old-time dance was in progress. The ceiling shook with the crash of feet and a noisy rendering of the Lancers.

Haynes was early for his appointment and he carried his glass to a corner table and studied his fellow customers to pass the time. They were a typical Saturday evening suburban crowd, a sprinkling of young couples but on the whole more men than women, more middle-aged and elderly people than young, more drinking beer than wines and spirits. The scene was cosy and friendly and pleasant till the door opened and the woman he had come to meet walked into the room. Behind her, moving with a smooth, sliding gait as if castors were screwed to the soles of his shoes, was the fat man from the station.

'The child is dead, Doctor. They stole my Mary from me, the welfare authorities and the police, and they gave her to those people to kill her.' Half an hour had passed and Anna Harb had finished her third double gin. She was a big, powerful woman with features as coarse as those of the cardboard guy Haynes had seen in the pram. Her fortune-telling business looked as if it paid well because her fur coat was black musquash and the long pin that held her hat in position was topped by a red stone which Haynes fancied was an Indian ruby.

'I have the second sight, Doctor. I make my living by what the ignorant call fortune-telling, and I know that Mary is dead and that is why they would not allow me into the hospital.'

'She is alive and physically well, Mrs Harb, but she needs your help badly.' Haynes forced himself to smile at the heavy face and shake his head at the constant repetitions. The noise of the dance thundered down through the ceiling, the room was hot and full of smoke and his head ached. The fat man had not been with Anna

Harb, as he had first thought, but was standing by the bar with a liqueur glass almost hidden in his great, flabby hand and surveying the assembled company with an expression of amused contempt.

'So you keep telling me, Doctor, and I will believe you when I see her.' The woman slipped back the coat, showing a low-cut dress and shoulders which were as muscular as a strong man's.

'You say that my daughter is obsessed by fire and dreams about flames and dying animals, that she may have caused a man's death because he lit a cigarette in her presence,' Anna Harb suddenly shook with laughter. 'Like mother like daughter, eh? A real chip off the old block, though I did better—I killed two men and a thing which called itself a woman. For over ten years I rotted in a stinking asylum till some nice kind gentlemen like yourself came and said I was sane and should be released. They let me out because of that, and I will always be grateful to your profession, Doctor. Even more grateful when you have filled my glass.'

'Of course.' Haynes crossed to the bar, glad of a brief respite. Apart from her grotesque appearance there was something repellent about the woman's personality which he had noticed the moment she had entered the room. It was like being with a big cat which remained contented as long as it were fed and constantly stroked. Hold back the food, though, withdraw the hand which gave pleasure and the claws would come out. He could quite understand her success as a fortune-teller. People respect those they fear, and Anna Harb had that rare quality, an element of terror.

'Another double gin please.' He waited for the barman to serve him. Some customers had left or moved their places and others had come in. Only the fat man remained completely stationary, surveying the room from his vantage point at the end of the bar as if studying a cageful of apes.

'Thank you, Doctor.' Anna Harb took the glass from him, the light winking on the ruby pin as she bent forward to drink.

'But why should Mary be obsessed with fire? We had no open fires in the caravan; only a gas stove and electric heating. Such a nice caravan it is and Mary was happy there with me. Sometimes her father would come to visit us. He is a Danish seaman with a wife in Copenhagen, but his ship was often in the Thames.

'Mary could have been taught my powers, too. I would have shown her the gift of the second sight and the way to look into the future.' A tear suddenly trickled down the dark cheek and she looked away from him. 'So much I could have done for my daughter, but they took her away from me. They said I was an unfit person to have care of a child because I was too fond of men. Is that a sin, Doctor Haynes?'

'Not a sin, though it may be disturbing for a small child.' A gift of second sight. Had the training for that been the original cause of Mary's sickness? Haynes considered what her lessons might have been. Drugs and hunger to produce hallucinations, hours spent in a dark cupboard or staring at the ink pool in the palm from which visions might appear. Added to such experience there would have been the constant stream of visitors. Strange men's faces on the pillow and the mother's beside them. 'This is your new Uncle Dick . . . or Gustav . . . or Kurt, Mary. Come and give him a kiss, darling.'

'But why do you keep repeating that the child is dead, Mrs Harb? I give you my word that she is alive and physically well.'

'Because I have seen her, Doctor Haynes. When that party of children came to London there was a newspaper story about it and a picture of them outside the hotel. It said how happy and fortunate they were and how some kind old people had renovated this lovely house in Scotland and prepared for their futures. I went round to that hotel and I waited outside. After an hour the children came out and I saw my daughter.' The woman lifted her glass again. She drank as if performing some strange ritual, and Haynes had noticed that it took her exactly three mouthfuls to empty each measure.

'Did she see you? Recognize you?' he asked, wondering if that were another link in the story—a sudden confrontation with the mother Mary had not seen for almost three years.

'No, but I saw her. I looked right into Mary's eyes and they told me her future. You may sneer at the supernatural, but I could read her destiny as clearly as print. It was ordained that Mary must die and the people who stole her from me were to be her executioners.'

'I have never sneered at the supernatural, but Mary is alive, Mrs Harb, and being well looked after.' Haynes lit a cigarette to conceal his feelings of impotence, and from the bar he saw the fat man raise his eyebrows as if the apes had performed some indecent antic. Giles Caitlin was the chief of the psychiatrists who had pressed for Anna Harb's release and he must have been crazy to do so. The woman was clearly paranoic and still potentially dangerous.

'Then you read about the coach accident, and when they refused to let you see her at the hospital you got the idea that she was dead. Tomorrow morning I shall take you to Saint Bede's and prove that she is alive.' He suddenly felt drained of strength as he made the decision. The shock of seeing her mother might give him a clue to Mary Valley's condition but it might also disturb her badly.

'And only then will I believe you.' The dark face was quite without expression, but her eyes stared straight into his with the terrible self-assurance of the insane. 'All the same, let us admit that she is alive for the sake of argument.' Anna Harb took her third and final drink of gin and pushed aside the empty glass.

'She dreams about a little room in a burning building, you say, Doctor? The door is red with heat and, outside, animals are being roasted to death. Where would my little girl have experienced such a thing?

'Very well, in the morning we shall go to the hospital, but tell me one thing now. You didn't think of Mary as just an ordinary patient, did you? There was something about her that frightened you.'

'We all fear things which we do not understand.' Haynes had noted the use of the past tense, but the woman spoke the truth. Every minute he had listened to that small voice whimpering from the pillow, every time he had played back the tape-recording had made him more and more convinced that his theory of racial archetypes was the only one that fitted. The memory of some-thing that had happened a long time ago was running through the mind of a child and it horrified him.

'But tomorrow we will see Mary together and you may help me to understand her condition.'

'We will do that, Doctor, if she is alive.' Anna Harb lifted her coat from the chair and stood up, but she made no move towards the door. She stood smiling at him and there was a magnetic quality in her eyes and her face and her whole body; a perverse attraction which made him understand her success as a prostitute. In spite of his earlier revulsion Haynes felt a sudden flush of animal desire for her.

'Now, let's forget little Mary and enjoy ourselves, Doctor. There is a bar upstairs which stays open till the dance ends at midnight. We will go there and drink together and you will dance with me. Then, after a time, you will not find me as unattractive as you do now.' A hand which had killed three human beings gripped his and she led him towards the staircase at the end of the room. Just before they reached it, she turned and smiled at him again.

'You will like me, Dr Haynes, that is a promise, but here is another: if you have lied to me, if I find that my girl is dead, I shall kill you.'

'Clark's Hotel. Is Lord Michael Fawnlee still staying with you, please? Thank you.' At the moment Anna Harb had started to lead Haynes up to the dance, the fat man had glided out of the bar and was now standing in a telephone booth.

'Good evening, my name is Forest . . . John Forest . . . and I wish to speak to Lord Fawnlee on a matter of some urgency.' Another voice had taken over from the operator and Forest pronounced his name as though it were as noteworthy as Shakespeare or Napoleon.

'I beg your pardon.' There had been a slight pause before the secretary spoke again and when he had finished Forest's sagging face flushed with anger.

'Your employer says that he has not heard of me and is not in the habit of accepting telephone calls from strangers? Then please tell him he should read the *Daily Echo* and that my business concerns a child who is supposed to be in his care.' Forest had been put out by the rebuff and he searched for a reprisal.

'Tell him to come to the phone at once please.' He remembered that Fawnlee was an active campaigner for total abstinence and the reprisal came to him. 'Providing that the old gentleman is sober enough to carry on a rational conversation, of course.'

Chapter Four

MICHAEL FAWNLEE was old and tired and he couldn't feel real anger nowadays. He had been irritated by Forest, but not annoyed because it was years since he had experienced any emotion except deep anxiety. He leaned wearily back in his chair, and as he listened to his visitor the memories of the long life which had made him what he was ran through his mind like water dripping from a tap.

Money and business and sweat, he thought. The knowledge that the first thousand was safely lodged in the bank and he could start on his own. The fun of planning and gambling and bargaining and watching one business grow into an empire; iron and shipping on Tyneside, jute mills in Glasgow, motor vehicles in the Midlands and two merchant banks in the City of London. It had been a benevolent empire though, he reassured himself. Not one of his companies had ever been hit by a serious strike and no employee had been deliberately made redundant.

Private memories too and so many of them. The intense love for his wife and the bitter disappointment when her hunting accident had robbed them of all hopes of children. Then Molly had died fifteen years ago, leaving him alone and without love, and the earlier memories, the frightening ones, had come back. Shiny black suits with their owners bent in prayer, his father's sermons and the texts on the bedroom wall always facing him. 'What a terrible thing it is to fall into the hands of the jealous God.' 'One careless act may wall you in Hell FOR EVER.' Nonsense, his adult reason had told him. The words of superstition and barbarism and insanity. But they had not been nonsense to a little frightened boy nor to an old man who thought he was soon to die.

But at last hope had come. Helen Van Traylen had talked to him and taken away terror because there was an escape from hell all the time and the Fellowship she founded was the way to it. Medical research came first, then the art collections saved for the nation, then the homes for the aged, then many more charities. A mountain of good works building up like Khama to appease the fierce God of the Middle Ages. Finally came the foundation of the orphanage and the comforting knowledge that salvation could be bought at a price.

'That is all you have to tell us?' He pushed memory aside and looked at his companions in turn. Sylvia Rheinhart, the widow of a textile millionaire, Eric Yeats, the retired Harley Street surgeon, George L'Eclus, the racehorse owner whose filly, Matapan, had won last year's Oaks. Old, completely trustworthy friends and fellow guardians united by Helen Van Traylen for the good of their souls. At the end of the table, lolling back as if the room, the hotel and the whole world belonged to him sat John Forest.

'By no means, my lord. So far I have merely recapped what you know yourselves and I am hoping you will give me permission to publish the story.' Forest had been a top Fleet Street correspondent for longer than he cared to remember. He had walked with kings and dictators and presidents and sheer power meant little to him. But he had an enormous respect for great wealth and there were at least three millionaires looking at him. Their mild, elderly faces awed him slightly, though he was careful to conceal it.

'The child, Mary Valley, is still at Saint Bede's Hospital, detained against your wishes. The injuries she received during the accident were superficial cuts and bruises, your own medical adviser at the orphanage stated that she is in good mental health and I have looked up this fellow Haynes's record which shows him to be a very unbalanced man indeed. Now, Sir Marcus Levin has confirmed this mysterious allergy and forced the magistrates to sign a receiving order. To me the whole business stinks to heaven and my paper would like to throw the book at Saint Bede's.'

'Which we do not want, Mr Forest.' There was a calm, authoritative note in Fawnlee's voice that, in the past, had cowed shop stewards and shareholders alike. 'There was quite unprofessional interference by Haynes as you have said, there may have been negligence too, but our Fellowship does not need publicity to support it. Providing the child is released as soon as her rash clears up, we have no further quarrel with the hospital authorities.'

Oh, haven't you? Forest smiled to himself, considering the information he had not yet revealed. Why are they so against publicity? he wondered. Is there something that they wish to hide? Perhaps Haynes had been correct all the time and Mary Valley was suffering from some serious mental illness which an inquiry might bring to light, and take her out of their care permanently.

'Do not think me impertinent,' he said, 'but is your doctor at the home a qualified psychiatrist? Is there any chance that Mary really may be disturbed as Haynes claims? After all the child's background is sinister to say the least and . . .'

'We do not discuss the backgrounds of our children, Mr Forest,' Mrs Rheinhart broke in. She was a small, dumpy woman who looked like a very nice maiden aunt; a knitter of socks and jerseys who would never forget a birthday. At the moment she was very angry indeed. 'Many of the boys and girls in our care come from sad and even criminal families, which is one of the reasons why they came to us and were not adopted into private homes. But they are all good, healthy children and Mary is one of the best of them. I forbid you to mention a word about her parentage.'

'Madam, I shall write nothing without your full permission.' Forest nodded and then glanced up at a big oil painting hung over the fireplace. It showed a tall, white-haired lady standing against a background of summer flowers and woodland, and he recognized her as Helen Van Traylen. She wore a white summer dress, long gloves reached up to her elbows, and though she must have been over seventy when the picture was painted, there was an almost girlish expression on her smiling face. Why should Fawnlee cart it about with him? Forest wondered. Out of mere affection, or perhaps as a talisman, a charm to ward off evil? The Fellowship really did appear to be in need of protection recently. To a gullible person it might seem as if some curse or supernatural conspiracy was directed against it. First the suicide of the Van Traylen woman herself, then old Colonel Anderson, another of the guardians, had fallen from a balcony, and at least two more violent deaths the details of which he would have to look up if he ever wrote the story. Finally this business of the child.

'I am on your side, Mrs Rheinhart. I want to help you recover that little girl by forcing the hospital's hand. My guess is that Mary will not be released as soon as you think. Remember that Marcus Levin is a good friend of Haynes and a contagious rash was the one thing Haynes needed to get the magistrates' order.'

'Mr Forest, you are going too far.' George L'Eclus had only a slight trace of a French accent. 'That rash does exist and you cannot suggest that Sir Marcus would deliberately infect the child. In any case, the dean has given us his personal word that Mary will be released in time to join the other children for our annual party in Scotland.'

'You have not heard of our party, Mr Forest?' Sylvia Rheinhart had forgotten her ill-temper and smiled up at the painting. 'As you know all our board of guardians are elderly and childless people with a great deal of money, and before Helen Van Traylen brought us together we were very unhappy people. But that finished long ago and now our Fellowship is what its name implies: a group of friends. We also feel that those children are our own and every year we join them on Bala Island and have a party in honour of our founder's birthday. All the children and all the guardians will be present, Mr Forest, and Helen Van Traylen will be there too in spirit, even though her body is dead. Do you think I'm foolishly sentimental to say that?'

'Not at all.' Forest inclined his head. The older people grow, the more they cling to dreams and become like children, he thought. Old Timothy Forsyte, who grew younger and younger till he was too young to live. Mrs Rheinhart was obviously looking forward to the party as much as any of the children and she had driven the details of her friend's death out of her mind. Helen Van Traylen had died horribly, and if her spirit did exist it would be a very troubled one.

'What surprises me is your lack of concern for Mary Valley's welfare. As long as the hospital releases her in time for this party you do not appear to care what happens to her. The little girl may be in good mental health as you say, but will she remain so after a few more days of Haynes's treatment?'

'There will be no more of that treatment.' Eric Yeats's hand rapped the table. Like many surgeons his fingers were as broad and powerful as a labourer's.

'I have spoken to Brian Plunkett, the dean of Saint Bede's, and we understand each other personally. I have his assurance that neither Haynes, nor any other trick cyclist will be allowed near Mary and I will be able to visit her at any hour of the day or night.'

'Then I would advise you to visit her yourself in the very near future, Dr Yeats.' Forest smiled as he prepared for the coming bombshell. 'Nurses and hospital porters talk as much as other people and it appears that Mr Haynes is a very determined man. From what I was able to learn at the hospital it appears that he is obsessed by Mary's case and because of this I made a point of following him last night.' The fat man lit a cigarette and inhaled greedily.

'Haynes led me to a public house near Thames Vale station where he met a certain lady. It was very noisy in the bar but as a young man I taught myself to lip read.' He blew smoke across the table and smiled straight into Fawnlee's eyes. 'Dean or no dean, my lord, promise or no promise, Dr Yeats, at this moment Haynes is probably introducing Mary Valley to her mother.'

John Forest had expected a strong reaction and he got it. Fawnlee choked with anger, Yeats hurled back his chair and hurried over to the telephone, the Frenchman gave a single bitter curse and Mrs Rheinhart made a sound which was part sob and part moan. Forest looked away from them and stared up at the oil painting. When he had first noticed it, he had thought how beautiful the sitter looked, but now the face appeared pinched and wretched as if she were trying to hide fear and intense suffering beneath a gay smile. He also wondered why a woman should wear such long gloves on a hot summer's day.

Chapter Five

'FOR CHRIST's sake, darling.' Tania Levin belonged to a growing school of women drivers who believed that thrust and charm provide the shortest distance between two points, and Marcus winced as the car shot straight out from a side turning into the path of a lorry. To his further embarrassment, she then bowed and smiled at the purple-faced driver as if imagining he had intended to jam on his brakes and give her courteous passage. 'Please remember that you're not only pregnant, but married to a highly important man of nervous disposition.'

'I'm not likely to forget either of those things, Mark.' Tania smiled fondly at the bulge of her belly. 'And stop quoting the Lord's name in vain, you cowardly Hebrew.' She accelerated to prevent a bus drawing out from the kerb and then leaned over and kissed him.

'The dean said you were to get over to Saint Bede's as soon as possible. "A matter of great urgency which I cannot possibly discuss on the telephone"—those were his exact words.'

'But he won't want to see me dead or maimed.' Marcus had recently heard that bad female driving caused more broken marriages than adultery and his foot was riveted on an imaginary brake pedal. Just what did Brian Plunkett want to see him about this time, he wondered. The more he thought about his deception, the less guilt he felt. If the child was as mentally ill as Haynes claimed, it was only right that she should have specialized treatment. There was no chance that they would be found out either. The Kaldorella cultures were virtually unknown in England and Redford-Smyth, the Van Traylen Fellowship's second opinion had agreed with his diagnosis of an allergic rash and that Mary Valley should remain in hospital till it had cleared up.

Yet he was both worried and depressed this morning. Marcus looked out at the grey streets of North-west London, seeing an old three-decker secondary school, a railway bridge, a block of flats towering gauntly like pre-war German barracks and everything enclosed by a dark, lowering sky with a promise of thunder. He had missed nothing by not going to Central Research the other day. The mutant they had slaved for six months to produce was just another failure; a weakling which was destroyed by the mildest of antibiotics. It had been largely his own brain child too, and its death seemed to herald a long run of bad luck.

'Here we are. Saint Bede's, safe and sound.' Tania's voice and a slur of gravel broke into his gloomy meditations. 'Should I come with you or get myself a cup of tea?'

'I think you'd better wait in the canteen, darling. Plunkett didn't sound as if he were wanting a social visit. And do me a favour, Tania. Move the car before you get several angry men after us.' He pointed to a sign that read 'NO PRIVATE PARKING—AMBULANCES ONLY' and hurried towards the entrance.

'Come in, Sir Marcus. Please sit down.' It was unusual for the dean to open the proceedings without the offer of a drink or a cigarette. He was standing in the centre of his study in exactly the same position as when they had last met, and Marcus had the absurd notion that he must pass the greater part of his day there.

'It's that blasted fellow Haynes and the Valley child again, Sir Marcus,' he said. 'A bad business from the start, and ten times worse now. Haynes has not only disregarded my orders, but he tells me that you support him in saying that the girl needs psychiatric treatment.'

'As I have no knowledge of psychiatry, I could hardly do that, Dr Plunkett.' Though Marcus still appeared urbane and untroubled he felt certain that his premonition of bad luck was coming true. 'Haynes talked to me about the child and played a recording of her reactions under narco-analysis. Mary seemed disturbed to me and, if she were my daughter, I would be glad for her to have treatment.'

'She is not your daughter, Sir Marcus.' The Badger broke in with a growl. 'Mary Valley is in the legal care of the Van Traylen Fellowship and I gave them my word that there would be no tampering with her mind while she remains in this hospital.'

'You gave Haynes orders to that effect?' Marcus was frowning deeply now. He had deliberately made a false diagnosis to protect Peter and give him time to study the case and the lie had been completely wasted.

'I did indeed. I told him that he must have nothing more to do with the child, that he must keep away from her, and I promised her guardians that my orders would be carried out. Now, it appears that Haynes has not only disobeyed me but that we—the hospital—all of us may be in very serious trouble.' Plunkett picked up his pipe from the desk and waved the stem towards Marcus as if it were a weapon: an old, grey, dog badger ready to do battle in defence of his lair.

'Earlier this morning I had a telephone call from Eric Yeats, who is one of the Van Traylen governors. He has definite information that Haynes still considers himself to be in charge of Mary's case and intends to continue treating her. Yeats finished by demanding that I suspend Haynes immediately.'

'Demanding!' Marcus raised his eyebrows. 'A strong word, Dean.'

'Possibly, but he has the whip hand. If I fail to agree, Yeats will either charge us with gross negligence or conspiracy, Sir Marcus.' Plunkett turned and stared through the window at the wide expanse of the quad. His father had been a senior consultant at Saint Bede's and he himself had studied and worked there for most of his life. Marcus knew that the hospital's welfare was his only real interest.

'Yeats finished by informing me that the Press already know the whole story and, unless Haynes is suspended by noon today, they will be allowed to publish it. The Fellowship will also demand a full inquiry into the nature of Mary's rash and why none of their other children were infected in the same way.'

'She was allergic to some substance I was unable to identify.' Marcus spoke confidently, but he didn't look urbane any more. An inquiry by experts might just stumble on the truth, and if that happened Peter Haynes would face possible imprisonment and certain ruin, while he himself would be regarded with suspicion for the rest of his life. He remembered how he had washed dishes every evening for four years while he had studied for his degree, the hard long road to a knighthood and the final recognition of a Nobel prize. Now everything might soon be wiped away and replaced by ridicule or worse. He could hardly be proved to have made a false diagnosis to protect a colleague, but he would be suspected of it till his dying day.

'So you stated, Sir Marcus.' Plunkett walked back to the desk and started to fill his pipe. His hands were long and thin and quite out of proportion to the rest of his body.

'You will naturally abide by that opinion and Redford-Smyth is bound to support you. But what am I to do? I am furious with Haynes, I dislike the man, but I don't want to ruin him. With his record of changing jobs in the past, suspension would probably ensure that he could never get another one in this country. At the same time, can we afford to tell the Van Traylen crowd to go to blazes? I have never liked publicity and I can imagine what the newspapers would make of a story like this.

'What the devil is that?' The dean had just struck a match but it dropped from his hand and lay smouldering on the desk. From the corridor outside came the sound of running feet and a child screaming at the top of its voice.

Plunkett was closer to the door, but he was a stout, slow-moving man and Marcus reached it before him. The first thing he saw was a nurse scrabbling on the floor and beyond her was a big, powerful woman in a fur coat. She was dragging a fair-haired child towards the staircase and the child was screaming and struggling in her grasp. There was mania in every tense movement of the woman's body, and as he ran towards them Marcus could hear the curses and half-formed sentences mingling with the child's screams. 'Damn you . . . You are not my Mary but a fiend; a soul that should not have been born. I shall send you back to hell, fiend.'

'Stop it. Let go of her.' They were at the top of the stairs when Marcus reached them. He grabbed the child's shoulder and the woman's arm at the same instant, saw a dark face contorted with rage swing round and glare at him, while Mary Valley's free hand clutched his jacket for protection. Then the woman drew back, her handbag shot out like a flail and for a moment the world went pitch black.

'You are all right, darling. She's gone and there's no need to cry any more.' As Marcus dragged himself to his feet he saw that the nurse had taken the sobbing child in her arms and was crooning over her. 'You're safe, Mary, and we won't let anyone hurt you again.'

'Are you all right, Sir Marcus?' Plunkett was staring anxiously up at him. 'You were out cold for a moment.'

'I can believe that. It felt as if there was a block of lead in her handbag.' Marcus pressed his handkerchief to a bleeding cut on his forehead. 'Did anyone stop her?'

'No, she got clean away down the stairs and across the hall.

Obviously a maniac and the porter has telephoned the police and given them her description. They're bound to pick her up without much difficulty, I imagine.

'Ladies and gentlemen, please clear this corridor and go about your business.' He waved aside a group of students and nurses who had appeared on the scene.

'Now, Nurse Rudgard, tell us what you know about this extraordinary business.'

'The woman was Mary's mother, Mr Dean. Hush, darling, you're safe now.' She held the weeping head against her bosom. 'Thank God you got to them in time, Sir Marcus. She was quite mad, shouting that she was going to kill the child. If you hadn't stopped her, I believe she would have done so.' The nurse stared at the deep well of the staircase.

'The mother.' Plunkett frowned. 'But how did she get in here? After that scene the other day I gave orders that she wasn't to be admitted under any circumstances.'

'Mr Haynes brought her, sir. I was busy in the linen cupboard and I saw them go into the room together. They were there for about half an hour and then I heard shouting and the woman came out dragging the child with her. I tried to stop her, but I slipped and fell. You saw what happened after that, gentlemen. Quiet, darling, everything is all right. I promise you.

'May I put Mary back to bed now, Mr Dean?'

'Of course, Nurse. But in another room for the time being. Give her a mild sedative and stay with her please.

'Haynes. Always Haynes.' Plunkett's face was a study in anger. 'He not only breaks my orders but must be completely insane. To introduce a criminal lunatic into the hospital and leave her alone with a child! I'll see that he never practises medicine again, if it's the last thing I do.'

'But did he leave them alone?' Marcus had started to walk back along the corridor. His head throbbed as if an animal were trying to gnaw its way out through the skull and he had to concentrate to keep his feet in line. 'The nurse was in the linen cupboard. She never mentioned seeing Haynes come out.' He opened the door and stepped into the little bright room with its flowers and gaily painted furniture and Beatrix Potter wallpaper. Two chairs were set beside the cot. One was empty but Peter Haynes sat in the other as if he were still staring down at a face on the pillow. His own face was white and vacant and there was a red spot like a Hindu caste mark in the centre of his forehead. It took Marcus a moment to realize that it was the knob of a long steel hatpin which had been driven into his brain.

Chapter Six

'WELL, well, Mark. Fame at last, my friend. This has brought you more publicity than if you'd discovered a means to prevent old age.' General Charles Kirk of Her Majesty's Foreign Intelligence Service beamed at the pile of newspapers on the Levins' sitting-room table. Five days had passed since Peter Haynes died, but as far as the Press were concerned he was very much alive. Anna Harb had vanished without a trace, and her appearance had been as much of a boon to the photographers as her history was to the reporters.

'No, she certainly would not be my cup of tea.' Kirk squinted at the heavy features glowering out from the *Herald* and picked up a copy of the *Examiner*.

'"KILLER OF FOUR STILL AT LARGE",' he read from the headlines. '"WHY WAS THIS WOMAN EVER RELEASED FROM BROADMOOR?" "HOME SECRETARY HECKLED AT MEETING." Humph, they might as well shout at a stone for all the attention Ivor Mudd will pay to that. Besides, his government weren't in office when Harb was let out.

'And here is something of a more personal nature, Tania.' Kirk put on his glasses to read the small print.

'But for the timely action of Sir Marcus Levin, K.C.B., F.R.S., Britain's most recent Nobel prize-winner, Mary Valley would almost certainly be dead. Nurse Mavis Rudgard, an eyewitness to the incident, told our reporter that the woman was on the point of hurling the child down the well of the

stairs when Sir Marcus arrived on the scene and rushed to
the rescue.

'Modest Sir Marcus himself claimed that he did nothing at
all remarkable, but his handsome, debonair face still showed
strain and the physical marks of the woman's vicious attack.'

Kirk grinned at the strip of sticking plaster on his friend's
forehead. 'Well, well. Modest Sir Marcus, indeed! I've always considered you the most conceited of men, Mark. Who knows? With
all this publicity the R.S.P.C.C. might give you some award to go
with your other decorations.'

'Publicity which I can well do without, Charles.' Marcus
was not finding Kirk at all funny. 'All I did was to pull the child
away from her and get laid out by a handbag of all things. But
these blasted reporters have been pestering me ever since it
happened.'

'The price of heroism, Mark. Thank you, my dear. I will have
one more very weak whisky for the gutter.' The general allowed
Tania to refill his glass. Though the room was warm he had not
removed his overcoat and a thick woollen muffler was draped
around his neck.

'Tell me, Mark, is this nurse's statement correct? Was Anna
Harb about to throw her own child over the stairs, or was she
simply trying to regain custody of her?'

'Naturally I can't say for sure.' Marcus frowned, once more
seeing the woman's face swing round and glare at him, hearing
her curses, and feeling the heavy bag crash against his forehead.
'But I think she intended murder, Charles. After all, we know she
had just killed Haynes and she was raving at the child. I heard her
say something about sending a fiend back to hell. Also that Mary
was a soul that should not have been born. I think those were her
words.'

'The devil they were.' Kirk's eyebrows came up in a white bar
across his forehead. 'How very curious because that's a quotation
from A. E. Housman concerning male homosexuality.' He raised
his voice and quoted pompously:

'Oh soon, and better so than later
After long disgrace and scorn
You shot dead the household traitor,
The soul that should not have been born.

'No, one would not have imagined that Mrs Harb would have been the kind of person to quote from "The Shropshire Lad". But let's see what that revolting fellow John Forest has to say on the subject.' The general turned to another sheet of newsprint.

'Now, Little Mary Valley is happy again and back with her playmates at the Van Traylen Home on the lonely Isle of Bala off North-west coast Scotland. She will play and sing and laugh again and forget her terrible experience.

'HAPPY, BUT IS SHE SAFE?' [He stressed the subheadings.] 'Anna Harb has already killed four human beings and is known to bear an insane hatred towards her daughter. Until this woman is in a place from which she will never be released, John Forest and the London *Daily Echo* are convinced that the child remains in the gravest danger.'

'Stupid, sentimentalizing, bloated, boring fool.' Kirk snorted and blew his nose with quite unnecessary violence. 'All the same he's got a point there. That woman must be found quickly.

'What did happen in that room, Mark? What set her off? By all accounts Harb appeared quite reasonable when she and Haynes arrived at the hospital, and the nurse heard them talking together in a normal manner. Why should she suddenly go berserk?'

'Apparently the child rejected her, Charles.' Marcus was wondering about Kirk's interest in the case. The old boy's job was foreign intelligence and one would have thought this murder was completely outside his province.

'For obvious reasons they have not questioned Mary very thoroughly, but her story is feasible enough. She said that she didn't recognize the woman at all, but was frightened by her appearance. Harb tried to kiss her and Mary screamed and clutched Haynes for protection. When he ordered her not to touch the child, the woman suddenly pulled out the hatpin and stabbed him across the cot.'

'She did not recognize her own mother after a period of less than three years? That sounds a bit unlikely to me, Mark. Could it provide a clue to the nature of this mental illness your friend Haynes kept talking about?'

'But I suppose we won't get any more information from Mary Valley. Because she is naturally distressed by what happened it was decided, rash or no rash, to send her back to the orphanage.' Kirk turned and massaged his hands before the electric fire.

'That deception could have got you into serious trouble, my friend.'

'I don't need to be reminded of that, Charles.' Apart from Haynes and Tania, Kirk was the only person who knew of his false diagnosis and Haynes was dead. Nobody would accuse him of anything and he was in the clear. All the same he felt partly responsible for what had happened and guilt and self-disgust were like the symptoms of a physical illness. Haynes had died, a child had almost died, and the last scene had brought everything back to him. An old, bent man hobbling into the bedroom and Mary Valley rushing into his arms.

'Uncle Michael . . . Take me home, Uncle Michael . . . Please don't let them keep me here to hurt me again.' Fawnlee had wept like a child himself when the dean told him that Mary could leave at once and kept thanking Marcus for saving Mary. There had been something immensely touching in the sight of those two figures, one bowed and old and the other young and dancing with happiness, moving hand-in-hand to the waiting taxi.

'Anyway, it's over now and we can get back to our own affairs.' Marcus left his chair and crossed to the window. The recent dull weather had blown over and it was a fine clear evening with the moon coming up across the river.

'I wonder if it is over, darling? Until that woman is caught, I agree with the newspapers that the little girl may still be in danger.' Tania was not looking at him, but staring hard at Kirk. 'I also wonder if this visit is an ordinary social call, Charles.'

'You have a most suspicious mind, my dear.' The general fumbled in his pocket and pulled out a cigar case with his left hand, which was a fin of scar tissue and lacked three fingers.

'You're right of course and I admit I'm not here merely for the pleasure of your company. I wanted Mark's eyewitness account of what happened at the hospital.' He lit his cigar and then walked slowly across to the table, obviously reluctant to leave the fire. 'The fact is that some months ago my department became rather interested in this Van Traylen Fellowship, and as you were very frank about your indiscretions, Mark, I'll put my own cards in front of you.' Kirk picked up his briefcase and laid it on the table.

'Yes, the Van Traylen Fellowship. A group of thirty people, mostly elderly and mostly rich, who have banded themselves together for charity. Who would wish to hinder, thwart, or even destroy such a society, Tania?'

'I don't understand.' She watched him take a bundle of photographs from the case and slip off a rubber band. 'Does anybody wish to destroy them, Charles?'

'It seems likely, but let me show you the little evidence there is.' Kirk laid the first photograph before them. 'Here is Mrs Helen Van Traylen, the founder of the Fellowship, taken a month before her death. A very remarkable woman indeed was Helen. I remember meeting her once just after the First World War and I don't think I've ever seen such a beautiful creature. Be that as it may, she married a disgustingly rich American named Vincent Van Traylen, and did not return to this country till after his death in 1950. She then got in touch with her old friends over here, Fawnlee, L'Eclus and the rest of them, and they organized this charitable body together. Medical research, the preservation of art treasures and ancient buildings were some of their aims, but the children's home was what mattered to them. The membership was restricted to thirty guardians and to ensure the loyalty and devotion of the staff they were included as equal members. Should a guardian die, the number of thirty remained because another person was at once recruited as a replacement. The qualifications needed are either money or some specialized skill which would be of use to the Fellowship. I have heard that the home on Bala probably offers the best educational facilities in the country. An extremely worthy body of people.'

'She remained very beautiful, Charles.' Tania was still looking
at the photograph of a white-haired old lady smiling gently at the
camera. There was a suggestion of both sadness and great strength
in the lined, but still youthful face.

'Not at the end, I'm afraid, Tania.' Kirk shook his head. 'She had
a malignant tumour and blew her brains out. A clear case of suicide; or so they said.' He laid down another photograph showing a
tall, thin man stretched out in a deckchair. The man wore a straw
boater, a blazer and what looked like an old Etonian tie.

'This is Colonel Paul Anderson who died nine and a half months
ago and brought my people on the scene.' Kirk paused to pull at
his cigar and finish the remains of the whisky.

'Anderson fell from the balcony of a nursing home where he
had been operated on for prostate gland trouble and was killed
instantly. My department was mildly concerned because, though
Anderson had retired last year, he had worked for Army Intelligence and was in possession of secret material which might be
worth a good deal of money in some quarters. I don't have to tell
you about that, Tania.' He gave her a little flickering smile.

'Because Anderson's death was dramatic we sent a man down
to hold a watching brief, and the police soon satisfied him that the
fall was a pure accident. As you can see from the picture, Anderson
was very tall and the rail of the balcony was only three feet high.
The police felt sure that he had leaned over and, being still weak
from the effects of the operation, lost his balance. Verdict: Accidental Death. I did not discover that he was one of the Van Traylen
governors till much later.'

'So what, Charles?' Marcus frowned up from the photograph.
'A woman with a malignant growth takes her own life and a man
loses his balance. Very sad, but why should you imply this . . . this
conspiracy against the Fellowship as a whole?'

'One reason is that I knew Paul Anderson, Mark. I didn't like
him, but I had to see a good deal of him professionally. The man
suffered from vertigo and he would not even go near the edge of a
railway platform for fear of falling. He also had a morbid terror of
dying. A strange thing for a soldier, but the very word death could
make him ill-tempered for the rest of the day. He was in the front

line from Africa to Germany during the whole of the war and I think he had seen too much of it. The thought of Anderson leaning over that rail is quite ludicrous.

'Helen Van Traylen and Paul Anderson. Only two reasons so far, but here are some more.' He laid out another three photographs. 'A child was the next. A nine-year-old boy in the Fellowship's care. His name was Billy Martindale and he went swimming from a beach near the home and was thought to have been swept out to sea. In any case the body was never recovered.

'Ah, I wondered if you'd recognize her.' Tania was staring at an obviously posed photograph of a stout, mannish woman seated before a typewriter. 'That is Naureen Stokes, the novelist; quite a prominent literary figure I understand, though I don't read historical romances. Miss Stokes had been spending a week-end at the orphanage and was on her way back to London. It was late at night and raining heavily and her car ran off the road and finished up at the foot of a cliff near Fort William.

'Finally another death by gravity and water. Elsie Kingsmill, deputy matron at Bala, who was fishing from a point near the orphanage, lost her balance and fell into the sea. Her body was washed ashore a week later, but Mr Kipling's "corpse-fed conger eel" had been at it and her head was missing.' Kirk bundled up his photographs and slipped them back into the case.

'That's that. All I can tell you. One charitable institution, five violent deaths within a single year and all the bodies which were recovered had been mutilated in some way. Now this horrible business of your friend Haynes and the Valley child.' He closed the case with a snap and returned to the fire.

'What's your verdict, my friends? Can Modest Sir Marcus offer any other explanation except coincidence and a run of bad luck?'

'That joke is wearing a little thin, Charles.' The Press reports had begun to give Marcus a persecution complex and he scowled at Kirk. He could not even enter his club without having drinks thrust upon him; colleagues slapped him on the back and only this morning the milkman had seized his hand in a crushing grip. 'All the very, very best, Doc. I promised my missus that I'd shake your mitt for what you did to save that little kid.' There was another and more cynical attitude in existence too, and yesterday he had overheard two students laughing about 'the chap who was laid out by a handbag.'

'It can only be a set of coincidences,' he said. 'People do commit suicide when they suffer from incurable diseases, cars do skid on wet roads and children are swept out to sea. But just where does your department come in, Charles? I thought their job was catching spies?' Marcus spoke rudely and he despised himself for it. Apart from the constant gnaw of guilt his temper had suffered since the death of Haynes and he was ready to take offence at the slightest thing.

'The department does not come in at all, Mark. Their interest ended with the coroner's verdict on Colonel Anderson.' Kirk stooped down and once again massaged his torn talon of a hand before the bars of the grate.

'As you know, I am semi-retired now and only hold a watching brief over a number of highly competent and trustworthy people who do not require any watching at all. I was bored out of my mind and that made me consider the Anderson case very thoroughly. Then, when I heard about the other deaths connected with the Fellowship I ceased to be bored and became very interested, very worried and very angry indeed.

'What about you, my dear? Do you agree with Mark that it is all pure coincidence?'

'There is not enough evidence to form any opinion yet, I think.' Tania's Russian accent was much more pronounced. Before her marriage to Marcus she had worked for Gregor Petrov, a departmental chief of the Soviet Secret Police and any problem of crime or violence fascinated her. 'All the same, five deaths and three of those people were very rich, weren't they? The Van Traylen woman, Anderson, Naureen Stokes. Would the word childless also apply to them all?'

'Clever girl. It would indeed.' Kirk waved his cigar at her in salute. 'All the Van Traylen guardians are without issue, to use a revolting term, and most of them are very rich indeed. Helen Van Traylen was worth over twelve million dollars at the time of her death, Anderson inherited fifty-one per cent of Eagle Textiles and

Naureen Stokes had ten bestsellers to her credit and had sold the film rights in two of them for over a hundred thousand pounds each. Even the poorest amongst them must be horribly wealthy. What would you say Eric Yeats was worth, Mark?'

'I don't know Yeats well enough for him to confide in me, but he is bound to be well off. He was not only one of the quickest surgeons in the country before he retired, but one of the most versatile. He once told me that he would tackle anything from a lobotomy to a kidney transfer.'

'Their wills, Charles.' Tania broke in excitedly. 'How did the people who died leave their money?'

'A good point, my dear.' Kirk straightened from the fire and pulled at his cigar. 'With the exception of the little boy and Miss Kingsmill, who only had her salary, every penny they possessed went to the Fellowship. Where a lot of money is at stake there is always a motive for murder, and if these deaths go on the Van Tray-len Fellowship will be one of the richest bodies in the country.'

'I see. Yes, I see what you're driving at, Charles.' Marcus's laugh was savage and bitter and he felt the cut on his forehead start to throb again. 'In the centre of the Fellowship sits the great fat spider; Fu Manchu disguised as Lord Fawnlee perhaps. He intends to liquidate all his fellow guardians and then make off with the loot. I suppose the little boy who drowned and Miss Kingsmill had somehow stumbled on his evil plans and had to be silenced.

'Or perhaps it is not just one spider, but a worldwide organization: the Mafia or a group of sinister Chinese with their headquarters at the bottom of the Pacific Ocean.' Marcus paced the room in his irritation. 'Please stop this absurd theorizing, Charles. The business is upsetting enough without that. We know Anna Harb was a lunatic who killed Haynes and attacked her daughter in a fit of mania. That cannot fit in with any plot to destroy the Fellowship itself.'

'I never said it did, Mark.' Kirk was looking at him with an expression of deep concern. 'I merely consider that five deaths, six, if we include Haynes's, are too many to be written off as coincidence.'

'They must be coincidental.' Marcus poured himself out

another drink, and as he did so he clearly saw the red stone glinting on Haynes's forehead. There had been so much death in his life, but this was one he was responsible for. As he lifted his glass, images of the past swam in the amber liquid. The charred bodies in the Warsaw Ghetto, shaven heads piled like mushrooms at Belsen, faces craning up from hospital beds and mouths pleading for life. 'Help me, Doctor. Please don't let me die. Please Doctor. I am not ready to die.' Finally the face which he tried so hard to forget but never succeeded in doing—Rachel, his first wife, burning in his arms, while the rain pattered over the Vietnam jungle and he had cursed God because they had no antibiotic to combat the little commonplace bug which was eating her up.

'You must have sent a hundred men to their deaths in cold blood, Charles, but now, because you're bored, you have become obsessed with this Van Traylen business.' There was a sharp crack, a stab of pain and he looked quite incuriously at the broken glass and the blood dribbling down his fingers.

'Stop it, darling.' Tania's arms were around him. 'You think you were the cause of Haynes's death, but there is nothing to feel guilty about. All you did was to help a friend.' She started to tie a handkerchief around his palm. 'Haynes contacted the woman and brought her to the hospital and he had only himself to blame for what happened.'

'Of course, Tania.' Marcus turned to Kirk. 'Please forgive me, Charles. What I said was quite inexcusable.'

'Not at all, Mark.' The general shrugged. 'You are right of course. I had to be cold-blooded in my job or I would have gone insane very quickly. You are probably correct in saying that this may all be coincidence too. Five deaths are not many when one considers how many persons connected with the Kennedy assassination have died and the official view remains that Lee Oswald was acting alone.

'Now, I'd better be getting on my way.' He picked up his case and started to move towards the door, when it opened and Jane McDoggart, the Levins' grim Scottish housekeeper, came into the room. She disliked Kirk and her frown made it clear that he would have been an unwelcome guest for dinner.

'More news of the case, Sir Marcus,' she said, laying an evening paper on the table. 'I told you that that puir, wee girl was not out of danger, just as I told you that hanging was too good for monsters like that Harb woman. I'm right as usual, it appears.' She smiled smugly as they craned over the newspaper. Banner headlines 'THE HUNTRESS' covered a full third of the front page and there was a picture of Anna Harb taken shortly after her release ten years ago. Beneath it was a brief report that a woman answering Harb's description had been seen on the ferry boat which made the crossing between the Scottish mainland and the Island of Bala.

Chapter Seven

THE room was windowless, completely air-conditioned and as antiseptic as an operating theatre. Fluorescent lights glowed bleakly from the ceiling, the walls were coated with anti-condensation paint and an electric sign prohibited smoking in vivid red letters. In the centre of the floor was a long steel table before which five girls were bent over machines which resembled oversized typewriters. The monotony of their work had given the girls slightly dazed expressions, and the machines made a hypnotic 'snick—snick—snicking' noise as they spewed out the sixty-four-row punch cards which were to be fed into the computer. At the base of each machine was a vacuum tube to remove the dust and the chads.

'We are now about to digest the material you have prepared for us.' Major Norbert Reilly gave Kirk and Tania a glittering smile as his assistant picked up the first batch of cards and carried them across to a metal box on another table. Until recently, Reilly had been in charge of the department's code and cypher files but at last his Ph.D. in electrical engineering had brought him up in the world. The powers that be had decided that automation should enter the intelligence services, and he had not only gained control of a computer which had cost the taxpayer more than a hundred thousand pounds but appeared to regard it as his own personal property.

'You mean that that thing is the computer, Norbert?' Kirk raised his eyebrows at the drab little box. This was the first time he had visited the major's sanctum and he had expected batteries of flashing lights and trembling dials.

'You are disappointed General? You hoped for something much bigger and more impressive?' Reilly chuckled against the snicking of the card punches and tapped his forehead. 'It's not the size, but what goes on inside that counts these days. Compare a modern guided-missile destroyer with a Second World War battleship, for example. Four thousand tons against fifty thousand, but the little chap is the far more deadly weapon.

'Microminiaturization is the plan for today and every cubic inch of that case contains more hardware, as we call it, than half a dozen conventional radio receivers, Lady Levin. At this moment thousands of integrated circuits are considering the general's problem at the speed of light and it is only the human factors that slow us down.' He looked sadly at Alsop, his assistant, and the card-punch operators. The material was piling up fast and Alsop was feeding the cards into a slot in the computer as nonchalantly as if he were posting letters.

'But will it give us an answer, Norbert?' Kirk repressed a scowl. Microminiaturization indeed! Hardware! Reilly knew that he detested technical jargon and had probably used the terms to annoy him. The fellow had been a good enough subordinate in the old days, but since the installation of this precious box of tricks he had grown decidedly too big for his boots. The constant repetition of 'we' and 'our' might be mocking references to the machine, but there was a hint of the grandiose about them too.

'That is up to you, General. It depends on the data you have given us. You wish to know whether some dark force is at work against the members of the Van Traylen Fellowship and whether the deaths of the past year and the attack on the child were part of that force's activities.

'We are considering the facts you have supplied, but we are a cold dispassionate brain, not a seer. The apparatus is programmed to solve problems which are essentially mathematical and allow no margin for error. The circuits are controlled by gates which reject everything that is inaccurate or inappropriate to the subject. If your data is full enough and exact enough you will be given an answer and a suggested course of action, but not otherwise.' He leered at Tania as if she had come to admire his etchings and then frowned as Kirk opened his cigar case.

'No, please do not light a cigar, General Kirk. That notice means what it says, because some of our circuits are so sensitive that any change of temperature or atmospheric conditions may affect them. As you of course know, the mean particle dimension of tobacco smoke is 0.6 microns.'

'Don't talk down to me, Norbert, or I'll have you back in "Codes and Cyphers" before you can say Michael Faraday.' Kirk growled as he replaced the offending cigar. 'So, it all depends on the fullness and accuracy of the information I gave you and which Alsop is now feeding into the computer.' He looked at the piles of typescript which the girls were transferring on to the cards and considered the miserable task he and his assistants had been engaged on during the past three days. They had sorted out every fact they could discover about the Fellowship and its members, living and dead, child and guardian alike. They had written reports on each of the deaths and given an account of every person who might have benefited from them. Finally they had put down all they could discover about Anna Harb and her associates. The police had found her account books in the caravan she lived in at the fairground and they made interesting reading. The fortune-telling business had obviously been very profitable indeed, and over twenty thousand pounds worth of blue chip securities were lodged in her bank, together with the deeds of six tenement houses in the East End of London. Apparently clairvoyance can deal with the past as well as the future, and what Madame Harb learned from her clients was often used for blackmail and the recruitment of teenage prostitutes.

Yes, he and his assistants had worked hard, but Kirk knew that the data was woefully inadequate and often based on hearsay. But there was nothing he could do about it now. The information was being considered by half a million transistors and all he could do was to hope that they would make something of it.

'Exactly, General.' Reilly was obviously quite unabashed by his rebuff and he nodded towards the girl at the far end of the table. She had transcribed all her material now and was leaning back in her chair with her eyes closed.

'And as most of the information has now been dealt with, perhaps you would like to try and think if there is any fact, however small, you might have omitted to give us.

'You too, dear lady.' Reilly had two gold bridges in his front teeth and they glinted in the cold fluorescent lighting. 'Anything that your good husband might have mentioned about Mr Haynes or the child or the Harb woman?'

'No, Major Reilly. General Kirk has already talked to my husband.' Tania had accompanied Kirk partly out of intense curiosity and partly to keep her mind occupied because she was very worried indeed. She and Marcus had been married for four years, but she had never known him to be so emotionally upset. The failure of the antibody was his own excuse, but behind that was the guilt which was eating into his mind like dry rot in timber. Guilt because Haynes was dead, guilt because he had broken his professional oath and, above all, guilt that he might have been partly the cause of making a mentally sick child even more disturbed. For the last three nights they had slept apart and throughout each of them she had heard him pacing the floor.

All the same, Marcus was probably right to sneer at Kirk's idea of a conspiracy against the whole Van Traylen Fellowship. Who would want to destroy a group of kindly old people and the children they cared for? Tania considered some of the theories they had discussed and rejected out of hand. Potential heirs, brothers and sisters, nephews and nieces, or old retainers who feared they were about to be disinherited in favour of the Fellowship and hired professional killers who had acted too late. Parents who had resented having their children taken from them and joined on a bent crusade against their new guardians. Even the old trick of committing several murders to conceal the motive for one. Not one of these notions made any sense at all. Haynes had been murdered by a solitary maniac and the other violent deaths must be pure coincidence.

'No, I can't think of anything else, Norbert.' Kirk shook his head. 'I'm afraid it really may take a seer, instead of your machine, to answer my question.'

'The Sphinx or the Oracle of Delphi.' Reilly spent twenty minutes under the sun-lamp every day and his smile gleamed against the tan. 'We are not that, I'm afraid, General. All we can do is consider, reject and supply an answer if sufficient valid data remains.' To Kirk's disgust, the major launched into a highly technical lecture on a computer's principles and five minutes had passed before he came to a stop. During that time, not a sound or a flicker of light hinted that the machine had been switched on. But, unlike Kirk, Tania could appreciate the mass of pulsing energy behind its drab exterior, with the circuits sorting and rejecting and storing at an unimaginable speed and then waiting patiently for Alsop and the operators to provide them with more information to consider. The scene made her think of a priest and a group of worshippers serving some primitive idol which would only speak when sufficient prayers had been offered up to it.

'Ah, that's it then, ladies.' Reilly saw that the last girl had finished and they got up and filed out of the room while Alsop fed her bundle of cards into the slot. There were two sharp metallic clicks to prove the apparatus was indeed alive and a strip of tape appeared from its base. Alsop rolled it up and followed the girls through the door.

'We've finished, General. Our deliberations are at an end; we have sorted the sheep from the goats and you may smoke if you wish.' Reilly pointed to the sign which had gone out.

'Alsop shouldn't be long, but as most of the problems we are asked to solve contain confidential information, the machine is programmed to work in code and the decoding device is kept in another part of the building.' He crossed smoothly over to a filing cabinet labelled 'Most Secret' and produced a tray of bottles and glasses.

'While we're waiting for Alsop, might we partake of some refreshment together. Dry or sweet sherry, Lady Levin? I know your preference, General.'

'Thank you, Norbert.' Kirk stared at the metal case as he took the glass from him. It looked so ordinary and harmless, and he was certain that though it was all Reilly claimed there would be no answer to his question, because most of the facts were inconclusive. All he had was a hunch and a suspicion that some immensely sinister force was at work against the Van Traylen Fellowship, and electronic devices did not follow any human hunch. All the same, at the back of his mind he knew he was right, and he could see the picture changing like magic lantern slides: a car lying crumpled at the foot of a Scottish cliff, a woman's face shattered by the blast of a shotgun, a tall man who feared death walking to the edge of a balcony, a child's body drifting out to sea and another child screaming in the grip of a maniac. Finally there came a picture nearer the present: old people travelling up to Bala to keep their founder's anniversary with the children in their care. Kirk was old himself and very fond of children. Somehow their protection seemed to be his personal charge and he prayed that the machine could help him to carry it out.

'It seems that there may be some information for you after all, General.' Reilly was looking at a telephone beside him. 'If the computer had recorded a complete blank Alsop would have rung through to me by now. Yes, we let you down as to appearances, I'm afraid, because you expected flashing lamps and whirring tapes and all the paraphernalia of a fruit machine, but it does appear possible that the residual material may have added up to some sort of conclusion after all. I must say that surprises me because most of the data was pretty vague.

'There you are, Alsop. Have we come up with anything comprehensible?'

'Not to me, Major.' The man ignored Reilly's outstretched hand and carried a sheet of buff-coloured paper over to Kirk whom he clearly considered to be his real boss.

'I don't understand this, General. Maybe it means nothing, because you gave us over thirty thousand words to consider and the machine has come up with less than fifty.'

He handed Kirk the paper and looked at him expectantly.

'Thank you, Mr Alsop.' The five lines of writing were in thick black type and Kirk did not need to put on his glasses. His face was

completely blank as he started to read and then two deep furrows
appeared at the corners of his mouth.

'Good God,' he said and his maimed hand trembled slightly.
'Your little contraption has confirmed my worst fears, Norbert.
This is what the Oracle has replied, Tania.' He handed her the
terse unemotional message which read:

VAN TRAYLEN PROJECT, PROGRESS TO DATE—SUCCESSES 4,
FAILURES 1—IN VIEW EXCELLENT RECORD, OPERATION TO
BE SPEEDED UP CONSIDERABLY—WITHOUT FURTHER DATA
IMPOSSIBLE TO PROGRAMME EXACTLY—SUGGEST AS FOLLOWS:
MEMBERS TO BE TREATED 5—METHODS, FIRE AND OR WATER—
DISPOSAL AREA, ISLAND OF BALA.

'Yes, my dear,' Kirk said, pulling himself stiffly out of the chair.
'This is exactly what I dreaded to be told. There is something, individual or collective, working against the Van Traylen people, and
in a few days' time they will all be assembled on Bala. When that
happens, five of them are to be murdered at one fell swoop.'

Four of them were already on their way. Lord Fawnlee leaned far
back in his corner seat in the railway compartment with Eric Yeats
beside him, and they both smiled at Mary Valley who lay half-
asleep with her head on Mrs Rheinhart's lap. Mary looked quite
peaceful and happy but they all knew the fears that were lodged in
her brain. The memory of that crazed, cursing woman dragging
her towards the well of the stairs and, beyond that, other memories which were just as horrifying. She was safe now, though, back
with her friends and protectors, and soon the reunion with the
other children would remove all fear for ever.

'Eight o'clock and we're due in at five past.' Fawnlee raised
the blind to look out at the Glasgow suburbs: tall tenements, a
ribbon of concrete highway and blast furnaces glowing like burning castles.

'Wake up, darling. This is Glasgow where we stay the night.'
Mrs Rheinhart raised the child into a sitting position. 'Then, in the
morning, off to Bala and home for good.'

'Home. That will be nice.' The little girl rubbed her eyes and followed Fawnlee's stare at the encircling city. She smiled at the road and the tenements and then the locomotive whistled, a gasp came from her mouth and her body shuddered.

'That sound,' she said, pointing out towards the glare of a furnace. 'The noise and the flames.' Her other hand grasped Mrs Rheinhart's for protection and her voice was a whimper. 'It was like that, just like that, when we burned the cattle.'

Chapter Eight

'NATURALLY the government are concerned, deeply concerned, ladies and gentlemen, but we must look at the situation in its true perspective.' Mr Ivor Mudd, P.C., M.P., Her Majesty's Secretary of State for Home Affairs, was a fierce Welshman with hair like streaks of black boot polish and a gammy leg earned while playing rugby for his country.

'I am the last person to deny that Mrs Harb must be found and found quickly, but I will not be bullied and these recent demonstrations have been quite inexcusable.' He rolled a malevolent eye over the assembled journalists and then turned to the secretary at his side. 'What did I say to you on the subject, Pomfret?'

'That the disturbances at your meeting last night were caused by hooligans, the rabble and persons with an uninformed fear of the mentally sick, Mr Mudd.' Pomfret was about to continue, but his superior waved him aside.

'Quite so. Also by elements who had been stimulated into hooliganism by the Popular Press. Which means you, my friends.' Once again Mudd's single eye glowered at his audience. Its neighbour was hidden by a cotton shield, having been put out of action by a well-aimed potato hurled across the Albert Hall.

'All the same, as I have said before, one must be realistic and I am not going to be coerced in any way.' He filled his lungs to deliver the slogan which had been largely responsible for winning him his majority at the last general election.

'My name may be Mudd, but it is quite certainly not Craven, or

Coward, or Cur. Everything necessary is being done to apprehend this unfortunate woman and I will not be forced into illegal action by anybody. Do you think I can be forced, Pomfret?'

'Most certainly not, sir.' The man took a step closer to the edge of the platform. 'Only last night, ladies and gentlemen, while in severe pain from his injury, Mr Mudd informed me that . . .'

'Minister, may I please ask a question.' This time Pomfret was cut short by the bitter, rasping voice of Carl Johnston of the *Daily Echo*.

'All of us here deplore last night's demonstration as much as you must do.' Johnston stared at the eye shield hoping that there was a real throbbing shiner behind it. 'We are also aware that your government was not in office when this "unfortunate woman", as you call Anna Harb, was released from Broadmoor. But the point is that she has killed four times in her life and is obviously a grave public danger. Surely the public should know what steps are being taken to apprehend her before she kills again.'

'The public do know, Mr Johnston.' Mudd's eye glared at him from a face which was laced with the blue marks of coal scars. 'Every police force in this country and on the Continent has a description of Mrs Harb and her picture has been circulated in the Press.'

'But is that enough, Minister?' Johnston pulled a copy of the *Echo* from his pocket. 'It appears probable that this woman is hiding on Bala and waiting for the opportunity to make another murderous attack upon her daughter. My colleague John Forest is now on Bala and he describes the island rather vividly:

'A wild, empty region of four hundred square miles with a human population of less than five thousand: the descendants of Celts and Vikings who settled there generations ago. A haven for sea birds and red grouse and grey seals; beloved of the mountaineer, the angler and the deer stalker. An island with a total police force of ten men and two women.'

'I have been given the necessary figures about Bala, Mr Johnston, and being a busy man who was born in a miner's cottage in the Rhondda, I take little interest in angling or the slaughter of inoffensive deer.' Mudd's hand rapped on his desk. 'Nor do I read the *Daily Echo*, though I have heard that Mr Forest has been writing clichés for so long that he has begun to think in them.'

'Then you should start to read the *Echo*, Minister.' Johnston smiled inwardly. The reference to the miner's cottage was always a sign that Mudd was about to lose his temper. With a little luck he might be forced into some really damaging statement. 'Whatever you may think of his literary style, John Forest has made it very clear that the Chief Constable of Bala has quite inadequate forces to search the island thoroughly and it is vital that both police reinforcements and the military are sent there at once.'

'Which I refuse to do.' The Minister's fist beat the desk a second time. 'I told you that I shall not be coerced in any way, ladies and gentlemen, and I mean just that. The very thought of sending troops to hunt down a single woman should be abhorrent to any civilized community and the government is in full agreement with me over this.'

'But Anna Harb is known to be insane, Mr Mudd, and has already attacked her child before.' The features editor of the *Informed Woman* put the next question. 'If little Mary Valley is in danger, surely you agree that any means to protect her would be justified?'

'In my opinion, no evil means can be justified, Miss . . . Mrs Marjoriebanks.' He had cocked an ear towards Pomfret for the information. 'But is Mary Valley in any danger? The island police are naturally keeping a watch on the Van Traylen Home and there is no real reason to believe that the woman is anywhere near Bala. The view of Scotland Yard is that the woman is most probably being sheltered by some of her criminal associates in London or has managed to leave the country.' Mudd rubbed his shielded eye which was aching painfully.

'Ladies and gentlemen, some of you witnessed yesterday's demonstrations in Trafalgar Square and elsewhere, and in view of Mrs Harb's mixed ancestry I would ask you to give this business the minimum of publicity from now on. We don't want any repetition of the Notting Hill race riots of some years ago.

'Yes. Mr Cornhill, I am aware that there are witnesses who claim to have seen Anna Harb on the car ferry to Bala.' Mudd had been a notable chapel singer in his youth and his powerful bass voice drowned the interruption.

'Two Irish labourers named Sean Connor and Desmond Joyce who were returning to Lochern, where they are employed on a building site, after a long week-end in Glasgow. Having seen her picture in the papers a good twenty-four hours later, they told the police that they thought . . . *thought*, Mr Cornhill, that they had recognized the woman on the boat. They described her as being dressed in a brown anorak and admitted that the hood covered most of her face. The only person who has paid much attention to this story is Mr Forest of the *Echo*, and it will take more than the *Echo* to make me send troops to Bala.'

'I think we should give the Minister the benefit of having expert advice, ladies and gentlemen.' Johnston was smiling at him in a most friendly manner now. Mudd had often lost his temper at other Press Conferences and he fancied there was a way to make him drop a really thunderous brick at this one.

'Connor and Joyce are young men with good eyesight, but I have naturally read my colleague's account and the time factors are not really in their favour, are they? The boys thumbed lifts from Glasgow and reached Torar ferry pier at midday on Monday. The next ferry did not leave till three o'clock and I'm wondering how they would have whiled away those three long hours.' Johnston gave a slight chuckle as he bowed towards the bench. 'I apologize for my early doubts, Minister. There does seem little evidence to support Forest's theory that the woman is on the island.'

'Thank you.' Mudd was always ready to forgive a repentant enemy. 'My friends, there is small cause to worry about Mary Valley's safety. The only evidence that Harb was on the island came from Connor and Joyce and I think we can discount that. The lads obviously found some nice, snug bar in which to pass the time and had had quite a few jars before the boat sailed.' His good eye gave a knowing wink. 'We all know the Irish, don't we?'

'Yes, Minister, we do know the Irish. Me mither was Irish.' Johnston was on his feet and there was a sudden brogue in his voice.

'Because Anna Harb has coloured blood you ask us to play down the story to avoid racial disturbances. It is you who are the racialist, Minister. Without any justification at all you have insulted a friendly nation and accused two young men of good character of being so intoxicated that they could not recognize a woman who was standing a few yards away from them. May I quote you on that, Mr Mudd?'

'You may quote me.' Pomfret was plucking his arm, but the Minister roared back. His black eye was becoming more painful every minute and Johnston's second change of face had infuriated him past the bounds of reason.

'Your miserable paper has blown up this business out of all perspective, Mr Johnston. There is no reason to imagine Anna Harb is on Bala and the evidence of Connor and Joyce can be completely discounted. They were probably so intoxicated that they couldn't even have recognized their own mothers.' He threw back his head and made the statement which almost led to his resignation.

'I refuse to be coerced by the statement of two drunken Irish hooligans.'

Four hours after Ivor Mudd blotted his political copybook the telephone rang in the Lochern police station. The caller was a local man named Angus McBride, employed by a construction company from the mainland who had been building a road across the north-east of the island. The work had ceased for the winter and McBride's job was to make periodic tours of inspection and see that the plant and other equipment was kept greased and free from rust. In one shed it appeared that he had discovered a vehicle that had no right to be there: a Dormobile with a London registration number. When the patrolmen arrived McBride had already forced the front door and was able to show them that the vehicle had been hired from a firm in Bayswater some five days previously. In the rear compartment, they found several items of female clothing including a brown anorak.

Chapter Nine

'CHECKMATE, Mark. You should concentrate more.' Kirk had already started to replace the pieces of his travelling chess set. 'If you had returned your knight to queen's bishop three a couple of moves back, this contemptible rout could have been avoided. I'll give you a rook next time.'

'Sorry, Charles, but I'm in no mood for chess at the moment.' Marcus was looking out of the window, seeing a line of beaches which were almost blindingly white under the early afternoon sun, brown mountains to the north and, out to sea, a jagged ridge of purple and blue which were the Cuillins of Skye. He leaned forward towards the driver whom they had engaged at Glasgow airport.

'How much farther is it, Mr McAdam?'

'Another twenty minutes will see us safely there, sir.' The man grinned at him through the mirror. 'I say see, but you'll most probably smell Torar first, I shouldn't wonder. A terrible stench the canning factory makes on a warm day like this.' He had driven with agonizing slowness since they had turned on to the narrow coast road and now pulled into the side to allow a bus to lumber past.

'Still, it's grand weather for the time of year; quite exceptional. Let's hope it stays like this for all your holiday, gentlemen.'

'Thank you.' Marcus turned to the window again. He had been born on the Polish steppes, spent most of his life in flat country and the sight of mountains usually excited him. But in his present mood he found this spectacular landscape merely sad and depressing. Glencoe, and Moidart and Skye, he thought. Memories of betrayal and massacre and little, bloody, unimportant wars.

Holiday indeed. He frowned at Kirk who had insisted on keeping the heater on, the windows tightly shut and was now engaged in lighting another cigar to thicken the already overpowering atmosphere. What a fool he had been to allow Tania to persuade him to accompany Charles on this completely fruitless journey to Bala. A change was not what he needed to forget Haynes's death. He knew that his nerves had been shattered by it, he knew that he couldn't sleep without drugs and his temper had become unbearable recently, but he also knew the cure: to concentrate completely on his work at Central Research and forget the whole unfortunate business. His wife and his old friend had been so persuasive that he had allowed himself to feel a slight thrill at playing amateur detective at first, but that was several hours ago. Now, as the car wound slowly on between the white beaches and the foothills, he felt nothing except self-disgust for his weakness.

Because it was crazy all right. There had been an official denial that Anna Harb was on the island and the whole business was a waste of his time. People died violent deaths each minute of the day and everything was coincidence. Kirk's fears were merely based upon a hunch and the reading of a computer which its own operator admitted was inconclusive. In half an hour they would be on board a ferry boat and the night would be spent in a small and probably uncomfortable hotel. The next morning Kirk proposed to call upon the assembled guardians at the orphanage and attempt to warn them of the supposed dangers. Marcus had little doubt that they would be received with ridicule or annoyance.

'What's the matter, Mark?' Kirk looked up from a map he had been consulting. 'The view not to your taste?'

'There is nothing wrong with the view, but I've never enjoyed a wild goose chase, Charles.'

'Neither have I, but in this case I sincerely hope that that is what we are on. The authorities share your present opinion that I am a senile busybody and that these people are in no danger, while all I have to support my fears is a hunch and the reading of Reilly's box of tricks. All the same, something tells me that the whole Van Traylen Fellowship is in very great danger indeed, and I am delighted that Tania persuaded you to play Watson to my Holmes.' He smiled at Marcus's scowl of fury and then raised his voice to admonish the driver.

'Mr McAdam, I quite realize that the road is narrow, the camber uneven and there are many blind corners. But would it be pos-

sible for you to drive just a little faster. I'm not asking you to be a
Stirling Moss, but perhaps you might risk thirty instead of twenty
miles an hour. My friend and I have a boat to catch, remember.'

'Don't you worry, gentlemen.' The man frowned sadly. 'When
you hired me in Glasgow, I promised me that I'd have you at Torar
in good time for the ferry and I'm a man of my word. Have a little
faith now.'

'Faith may be an excellent thing in religion, Mr McAdam, but
it has no place in modern transport.' Kirk glowered at the stolid
back, but he might have been talking to a stone statue.

'Just you relax and enjoy the view, sir, and rely on Angus
McAdam. There's the boat putting in now.' He nodded towards
a little red-funnelled steamer disappearing behind a promontory
to the north. 'Takes her a good fifteen minutes to turn round and
berth and you'll be able to smell Torar at any moment.'

'I can smell it now.' As the car topped a rise, a stench of rotting
fish came through the heater vent and the general pulled hard at
his cigar. The sun was just starting to sink towards the west and
mist was rising in spirals around the ridges of the Cuillins. Somewhere behind them lay the Island of Bala and journey's end.

'So we can, sir, which means there's no call to hurry.' McAdam
slowed to a walking pace to give way to a convoy of three cars and
a lorry which had been crawling behind them.

'Safe and sound, gentlemen, that's my motto, and it's the only
one for the road. Let the other fools break their necks, if they've
a mind to.' He changed into second gear and the car proceeded
down a final hill into the town.

Though Torar was small, there was an aura of grandeur and
self-sufficiency about the place which made it a real town or even
a miniature city, complete in itself. They crawled past a repertory
theatre, a court house, two banks, a customs house, the offices of
the *Inner Isles Clarion and Daily Advertiser* and the Municipal Buildings: a noble pile of nineteenth-century Gothic with two statues
before its portico. One showed Prince Charles Edward Stuart
gazing soulfully out towards Skye, and his neighbour was Queen
Victoria crouched in widow's weeds with a sour look on her stone
face.

'Here we are, gentlemen.' McAdam drew up alongside a broad quay, white with bird droppings, and got out to open the door for them. 'Safe and sound and in plenty of time, as I promised.' Drifters were tied up alongside the quay and crates of gutted fish were being loaded on to lorries. To the right lay the source of the smell which had troubled them from a mile back. A line of corrugated iron sheds, each proudly bearing a notice that they were the home of PURRY PUSS CAT FOODS which KEEP PUSSY PURRING. Sea birds wheeled and screamed overhead, and at the end of the quay the red-funnelled steamer had just tied up. A lift was raising cars from its lower deck and passengers were walking down the gangway.

'Seven pounds was what we agreed on, Mr McAdam.' Kirk hated slow driving and he brought out his wallet with a show of ill-humour. 'And that was to include your tip, I remember.' He handed over the notes reluctantly and then swung round as a great flabby hand touched his arm.

'What a pleasant surprise! General Kirk of Foreign Office Intelligence in person, and Sir Marcus Levin, our most recent Nobel prize-winner.' John Forest beamed as if they were old, much loved friends whom he had missed badly.

'The plot thickens.' Forest turned to a foxy-faced youth at his side. 'While I'm talking to these good gentlemen, Alfie, please nip over to the *Clarion* and see if the office has sent any message for us.

'Now, may I ask what brings you to these distant shores, gentlemen?'

'You may ask, Mr Forest, but our business is purely personal and I have no intention of telling you what it is.' Kirk had drawn back hurriedly because John Forest repelled him in the way many people are revolted by certain animals or insects.

'Don't be like that, General.' Forest shrugged his fat shoulders and tapped a copy of the *Glasgow Herald*. 'What about you, Sir Marcus? Are you here on another errand of mercy perhaps? A further gallant attempt to defend your protégée, Mary Valley? Have you seen the publicity I've been giving her, by the way? My articles are being syndicated all over the world and have already brought in a good deal of money for yours truly.'

'One could hardly miss them, Mr Forest.' Marcus did not share

Kirk's horror of the man, but there was no doubt that he was a public nuisance and it was largely his efforts that had kept the story alive. Forest had at first recounted the lurid details of Anna Harb's background and then hurried north to create the necessary atmosphere. A warm, friendly house full of laughing children, but one child who did not laugh any more because she was waiting. A little fair-haired girl who kept looking towards the doors and the windows, staring out at the dark glens and the mountains because she knew they were the hiding places of the woman who had sworn to kill her. Forest had aired much superficial knowledge of telepathy and extra-sensory perception and quoted cases of other children who had been linked to their parents by closer ties than blood. Mary Valley must know that her mother was on the island and her recurring nightmares were most probably of something that had happened to Harb herself long ago.

'I wondered why they allowed you to publish such sensational rubbish, Mr Forest.' Kirk had gone over to the ticket office and Marcus waited impatiently for his return. 'Is there any truth in your claim that the woman is on Bala?'

'I haven't the slightest idea, Sir Marcus.' The fat man's chins joggled as he spoke. 'But I should say it's highly unlikely. Bala is a wild, deserted island with plenty of cover, but the arrival of the ferry at Lochern usually attracts sightseers and I should have thought a woman of Anna's distinctive appearance would have been noticed.

'By the way did you hear the latest news? It appears that Ivor Mudd lost his temper at a Press Conference and blurted out that Connor and Joyce were as tight as ticks and couldn't possibly have recognized anybody on the boat. A political clanger by Mr Mudd, but I wouldn't be surprised if he wasn't correct.' Forest nodded towards a public house just visible behind the canning factory. 'According to a most reliable source of information, the lads spent three happy hours in the Cameron of Lochiel over there and knocked back at least eighteen pints of warm, gassy beer before the boat sailed.

'No, I shouldn't think Madame Harb is anywhere near Bala, but will be hiding out in some rat hole in London. All the same I'll always be grateful to her and her daughter for the story. An unpleasant child Mary, Sir Marcus. I watched her at the anniversary party they had at the orphanage and I've never seen such a smug, self-satisfied little brat. Whatever your pal, the late lamented Peter Haynes might have thought, I wouldn't have said there was a scrap of neurosis in her.'

'The party was yesterday?' Kirk had returned with the tickets and he raised his eyebrows. 'I thought tomorrow was the date.'

'It was to have been, General, but they put it forward a couple of days. L'Eclus told me that some of them had business appointments which couldn't wait. What a bore that man is! It was open house for everybody and he gave a long, pompous speech to children, fellow guardians and visitors and then followed it up with conjuring tricks. One thing I can tell you: the Van Traylen people themselves have no fears of the sinister Anna making a further attack on their unpleasant charge.

'Private business, eh, gentlemen?' From the end of the quay the steamer gave a long mournful whistle and Forest smiled at their suitcases. 'I thought the story was dead, but now two distinguished personages arrive on the scene and I begin to wonder.' His eyes flickered from the boat to the car park of the Lochiel.

'Should I go back to civilization as I intended, or is there further work for me on Bala? Let us see what the Fates suggest.' He rummaged in his pocket for a coin and then frowned as his assistant came running along the jetty towards them.

'What zeal, Alfie,' he said. 'I never thought you could move so fast. Well, what is it boy? Has Mafeking been relieved? Has war broken out? Has the Almighty sent us a personal message of congratulation?'

'No, sir. There was no message from the office.' Alfie was obviously badly out of training and the words came gasping out as if he had been strangled. 'But it is true, Mr Forest. Every word you wrote is true.' There was adoration in the little foxy face. 'The Courier's correspondent at Lochern just telephoned through to them. The police have been examining an abandoned car; a Dormobile and . . .'

'Guess whom it belonged to, gentlemen?' Forest had grabbed a scrap of paper out of his henchman's hand and he beamed

triumphantly at Kirk and Marcus. 'Well, well, how very extraordinary. Those two Irishmen were telling the truth after all and it
seems certain that Anna Harb really is on that island. I never really
believed Connor or Joyce for a moment and merely had a hunch.
Perhaps Harb is not the only one with second sight.

'Your admiration does you credit, my boy, but there is work to
be done.' He nodded at Alfie, who was staring up at him as if he
had just witnessed a miracle. 'The fleshpots of London are not for
us, so go and recover our dunnage.

'Sir Marcus . . . General Kirk, perhaps I might have the pleasure
of buying you a drink on board.' He gave them both a sweeping
bow and moved off towards the ticket office.

'I agree, Charles, a horrible fellow, but a competent one. You
have to grant him that.' Forest had gone straight down to the bar
and Marcus and Kirk stood on the boat deck as the ferry rounded
the headland and met the first swells of Bala Sound. In the gathering twilight, the Cuillin range still dominated the horizon, though
its peaks no longer looked beautiful, but black and threatening like
jagged teeth grinning above the layers of mist.

'I suppose he's competent enough.' Kirk was standing with his
back against the funnel cowling which was pleasantly warm. 'Do
you agree that we were right to come now, Mark?'

'Quite the opposite. We know that the woman is on the island;
a single maniac who will be hunted down like a wild animal.
The government are bound to send police reinforcements and
troops now and all we shall see is a witch hunt; men and dogs and
machines against a single, insane woman. I know it is necessary,
but I don't want to be part of it.' Marcus steadied himself as the
little ship rolled on the swell. 'Do you remember Gustav Holzach?'

'Naturally. He was an S.S. war criminal whom they arrested in
Munich five years ago. Weren't you at the trial, Mark?'

'I was. They made me give evidence against him.' Marcus was
staring aft at the boiling wake. 'Holzach was in charge of a transit
camp for slave labourers in the Ruhr and I was one of its inmates
for a time. When they arrested him he was living in a Bavarian
village, the headmaster of the local school, universally liked and
respected with a wife and three young children. I had seen Hol-

zach in action, Charles; felt his whip, watched him beat a woman to death with a pick handle, heard him laugh while he did it and I was delighted to testify against him. Yet, when he was brought up into the dock, so much older than when I had last seen him, so changed and so very very frightened, my only emotion was extreme pity.'

'Which does you great credit, my friend, but is hardly appropriate to this case.' A sailor had emptied a bucket of galley waste overboard and Kirk raised his voice against the screams of the gulls. 'We now know that Anna Harb is on the island and the chances are that she will soon be found and made to talk. When she has talked, I think that even you will be convinced that she is not merely a solitary lunatic but the pawn of some organization which is working against the Van Traylen Fellowship as a whole.'

'It is not I, but the Van Traylen people you need to convince, Charles.' Marcus felt both irritation and deep anxiety. Kirk really did appear to be growing senile, he thought. He himself had seen Anna Harb, he knew she was insane, but his old friend had spent most of the journey from London discussing a dozen theories, each more untenable than its predecessor.

'I must convince them, Mark.' The general was rubbing his torn hand up and down against the cowling. 'As you know I have spoken to three of them already; to Fawnlee, to the Rheinhart woman, to George L'Eclus, the racehorse owner. They all sneered at my warnings, but I could sense that each one of them was hiding something and was very frightened indeed. Yes, maybe it was blind instinct, Mark, but I am certain they know that those deaths were not simple coincidence, but for some reason refuse to admit it.'

'And you think that if you get them together in a body you might be able to persuade them to take your warnings seriously?' A sudden picture of Kirk standing before the assembled guardians like a schoolmaster before his class flashed through Marcus's head. The old boy really was losing his grip. According to Forest, these people had no anxieties and they were all rich and powerful with years of authority behind them. Short shrift was the expression to describe the hearing he would probably get.

'I don't think, Mark. I hope. But if I can get them together, I believe I may be able to break through the barrier. You are still comparatively young, you see. You can't appreciate the inevitability of death.'

'Can't I, indeed.' Marcus raised an eyebrow. 'I am a doctor of medicine, remember, and I survived both the Warsaw Ghetto and Belsen. I also watched my first wife die of yellow fever.'

'I'm not denying that you've seen more death than most men, Mark. But there was always hope, wasn't there? A hope that the Red Army might advance on Warsaw; that you might survive Belsen, as indeed you did; that Rachel would throw off the fever. You can never have experienced the feeling of complete impotence and utter inevitability which one gets at my age. The certain knowledge that one's organs are running down and degenerating and nothing can stop the process; lungs, liver, kidneys, and the heart. The only merciful thing is that the brain cells are decaying too and weariness helps one to accept the approach of the last enemy.'

'And so?' Another island, Raasay, was in view beyond Skye, and to the north of Raasay, Marcus could see a line of white which was the beaches of Bala.

'So, one does not fear death for oneself, Mark, one accepts and may very often welcome it. All the same, old people search for immortality. A religious faith is probably the best way and after that come children. As you know, I had two kids once; a boy and a girl. They died during the war and, until recently, I imagined I had got over it. Now, as the years go by, I find myself thinking about them more and more.' Kirk was staring straight out over the bows. Beyond Raasay and Bala lay the Atlantic; empty water all the way to the Nantucket light. Marcus knew that Kirk's son was somewhere beneath that ocean; a cinder in the boiler room of a torpedoed cruiser.

'What you are saying is that these people are too old to take much interest in protecting their own lives but seek a sort of vicarious immortality from the children in their care. If you can persuade them that the children are also in danger; that the little boy was not swept out to sea accidentally, that Anna Harb was deliberately provoked into attacking her daughter, then they may pay attention to your warnings.'

'I said I hope that they will. From the talk I had with Fawnlee, it seemed clear that those children provide their main purpose in living and . . .' Kirk broke off and swung round scowling. Like many stout men, John Forest could move like a cat and the gulls and the beat of the engines had screened his almost silent approach from behind the funnel.

'You have been eavesdropping?'

'You might call it that, General Kirk, though the term is not very appropriate at sea, I would have thought.' Forest leaned comfortably back against a life belt and beamed at them.

'May I ask the nature of this sinister organization which threatens the Van Traylen Fellowship, gentlemen? This appears to be my lucky day. Anna Harb made a good story, but your notion is far more exciting, General. Like Saul I went to look for asses and may have stumbled on a kingdom.

'Please do not throw the Official Secrets Act at me, General.' Forest shook his head gently. 'You are here as a private individual and you can't use that against me.'

'No, not the Official Secrets Act, Mr Forest.' Kirk's face was flushed. 'All the same, I have many good friends in Fleet Street and Lord Dillmayne, the proprietor of your paper, is a member of my club. If you publish one word of our conversation I think I can make things very hot for you.'

'I'm quite sure you could, sir.' The fat man still smiled but his voice was suddenly serious.

'But why should you want to stop me publishing your suspicions, General? If some force really is at work against these people, surely the facts should be made public?' He raised a fin-like hand and pointed up the channel. Lochern, the tiny capital of Bala, was in plain sight and, to the right of it, a fishing boat or a big cabin cruiser was coming towards them, her bow wave just visible in the falling dusk.

'If you had taken me into your confidence earlier, gentlemen, I could have saved you a lot of trouble. You want to talk to the Van Traylen guardians in a body, but you are too late. The anniversary party is over, General. Inver House has its own private jetty and that launch, the *Niobe*, goes with it. Our friends appreciate privacy and obviously consider the ferry is for the herd. I could have shown you a convoy of Rolls Royces waiting in the car park to meet her.'

'All the guardians are on board that boat?' Kirk stared at the launch and he felt a sudden sense of defeat. Was Marcus right and they had come on a wild goose chase after all? He had been certain that the computer's verdict was correct and something was planned to happen on Bala. But there were the intended victims returning peacefully to the mainland to carry on their normal affairs. The Ides of March appeared to have gone and his fears might well be groundless.

'I've no idea how many of them are on board, General. All I know is that that's the orphanage launch and several large cars are waiting for her at Torar.' Forest was watching the boat with unconcealed envy. It was approaching fast, but hardly rolling at all on the wide swell.

'A very nice job, isn't she? Twin Thorneycroft diesels, I've heard, which give her over thirty knots. Stabilizers, radar, lounge, sleeping accommodation, the lot. All fitted out by Walkers of Poole. No expense spared by our friends of the Fellowship.'

'But they are not making for the mainland.' Marcus could see that the bows were pointing straight towards the ferry and the launch was obviously heading towards Raasay on her starboard quarter.

'They must be, Sir Marcus. This channel is a maze of navigational hazards: snags, half-concealed rocks, freak currents. Her skipper is merely avoiding one of them.'

'Like hell he is.' Marcus's words were drowned by a bellow from the ferry's whistle and the deck lurched under his feet.

'It looks to me as if she's trying to come alongside.' The launch was very close now, still heading straight towards the steamer, and Marcus could see a Royal Yacht Club burgee stiff at her mast head and hear the roar of the diesels on the following breeze. He reached out to help Kirk steady himself as the ship's engines shuddered into reverse and she swung hard over to port.

'Charles, I think you may be right after all. That boat is in trouble and they're coming to us for help.' Again the whistle bellowed in protest, but the launch did not slacken speed or course. 'Either the controls have jammed or she's sinking.'

'No, she's not sinking, Mark.' Kirk's hand was stretched against the cowling like the claw of a bird. 'Look at the smoke, though.' Less than thirty yards separated the two vessels and he could see that the grey plume he had thought to be exhaust was not coming from the funnel.

'Get down while you can. Those poor devils have had it.' He grabbed Marcus and Forest by the arms and flung himself forward. As their bodies touched the deck the sky flashed bright orange.

Chapter Ten

'You gave us a straight tip, the clearest possible warning, General Kirk, and we refused to take it.' Captain Archibald Miles Sinclair Cameron, Earl of the Inner Isles, Hereditary Lord and Chief Constable of Bala, Keeper of the Silver Cross of Saint Columba, R.N. Retd., brought a gnarled fist crashing down on his desk. He was a thickset, leathery man with a face that was tanned more by spirits than sun and wind, and his heavy-lidded eyes glowered across the charge room of the Lochern police station which was packed far above its comfortable capacity. A uniformed inspector stood by the door, Kirk and Marcus and a young naval lieutenant were squeezed on to a narrow bench and the only other chair was occupied by Eric Yeats, who sat hunched far forward with his eyes riveted to the floor like a man in a state of extreme shock.

'You warned us, General. You telephoned Inspector Grant and you wrote to me personally. You told us that some event might take place and we paid not the slightest attention to you. Because of that six people have died; the worst single tragedy this island has suffered since the '45.' His bloodhound eyes stared out of the window opposite the desk. The little square outside was largely composed of churches—Catholic, Anglican, Presbyterian and Free Church of Scotland. Next to the Anglican establishment stood a crumbling, seventeenth-century building, gay with fuchsias at its base, grim with barred windows; the old jail house from which his ancestors, the fit and the wounded, lord and retainers alike, had been marched out and publicly hanged by Butcher

Cumberland's troopers over two hundred years ago. On the hillside beyond the buildings, tents and prefabricated huts were being busily erected. The evidence of the Dormobile and the anorak had forced Ivor Mudd's hand and soon soldiers would move in from the mainland.

'I don't think that you or the inspector need reproach yourselves, My Lord. After all, the Home Office refused to listen to me and my anxieties were largely intuitive.' Kirk spoke slowly because the events he had witnessed still distressed him. The smoke oozing out from the launch, the gout of orange flame and a scream of pain from John Forest. Then, when he and Marcus had pulled themselves to their feet, nothing except a drifting grey cloud and timbers leaping out of the sea as if on springs. 'All you received was the warning of a private individual and you had no reason to take it seriously.'

'We had every reason, General Kirk. We knew of you by reputation and events have proved you correct. But please don't address me by that wretched title. I'll answer to Captain, or Chief Constable, or just plain Cameron, but My Lord makes me feel like a blasted bishop.' The laird pulled out a large purple handkerchief and blew his nose with quite unnecessary violence.

'Now, let's hear from you, Lieutenant. Your people have only managed to recover the fragments of three bodies to date and I gather it's unlikely they'll find any more.'

'Highly unlikely, sir. As you of course know, the tide runs through that sound like a mill race. The rest of the bodies and all the floating wreckage will be far out in the Atlantic by now. We've got divers looking for the hull of course, but they won't be able to go down if the weather breaks, and the barometer is falling.'

'Quite so. The hull was metal, I take it?' Cameron nodded. 'And from the small amount of wreckage you did find it was impossible to discover if the vessel was sabotaged or how it was done.'

'Completely impossible, sir. Our first thought was that a wartime mine might have been responsible; we're still finding them along this coast, but the eyewitness accounts ruled that out at once. I have a theory about the sabotage, but it may not hold too much water.'

'Well, let's hear it, man. Any theory is better than nothing at all.'

'Of course, sir.' The young officer was looking nervously at Yeats as if reluctant to disturb his grief. 'If it was sabotage and the saboteur knew her business, the problem of explosives might not be difficult. There was a small dynamite store in the shed where the Dormobile was found and, though he has no inventory, the caretaker considers that some cartridges and fulminate detonators are missing. Very lax behaviour on the part of his employers, but there you are.' He shrugged, still looking towards the bowed figure of Yeats.

'No, the explosive would not have been the real worry. Many bank robbers have stolen dynamite from quarries and so on. But the timing mechanism must have been complicated. Remember that Mrs Harb could have had no idea when the launch would next be used.'

'That's jumping the gun a bit. We've still only a suspicion as to who this saboteur is.' The Chief Constable had been up all night and he did not trouble to conceal a yawn. 'All the same, you're beginning to interest me, so go on, boy. What timing device would operate, not only when the launch was next used but ensure that she had reached the open sea before blowing up?'

'The fuel system, sir.' The lieutenant turned to Yeats. 'Doctor, am I right in saying that the launch was piloted by Mr L'Eclus who intended to return to Bala that same evening after landing the five other guardians who were on their way back to London?'

'Thank you.' Yeats had answered with the slightest nod of his head and he continued: 'Is it also correct that you kept supplies of petrol at the orphanage jetty but no diesel oil and Mr L'Eclus intended to refuel at Torar?'

'I believe so. I think I remember George saying that there had been a leakage of oil from the main supply, but I'm not really sure.' Yeats's voice had a slight stammer. 'No, I'm sorry, but after what happened I just can't remember anything clearly.'

'If the fuel tanks were low, L'Eclus might have switched over to the reserve during the crossing.' Cameron stood up and paced the narrow strip of floor as though it were a quarter deck. His legs were very short below his kilt but he had a chest like a gorilla and still swung a hammer to open the local highland games.

'Yes, I see your point, Lieutenant. There is no diesel oil at Inver House, but plenty of petrol. If somebody had drained the second tank, refilled it with petrol and wired detonators and a stick or two of dynamite tightly against the engine, what would have happened when the reserve switch was operated?'

'In my opinion exactly what did happen, sir.' The officer consulted a notebook. 'I telephoned the *Niobe*'s makers and they confirmed my suspicions. The switch to the reserve supply is automatically controlled and comes into operation once the main tank contains less than a gallon of fuel. For approximately ten minutes after that the engines would be running on a mixture of petrol and diesel fuel and simply produce an abnormally high power output which might not be noticed by the coxswain. But once neat petrol reached the combustion chambers, the cylinder head gaskets would either expand or be blown open and the dynamite detonated.'

'And she would go up in just the way she did.' The laird nodded approvingly. 'My congratulations, Lieutenant Reed. An intelligent theory and probably the correct one.' Once again his handkerchief came into operation.

'It is also supported by information which Inspector Grant received some time back but ignored. Tell General Kirk about that, Inspector.'

'Of course, Chief Constable, though I have no guilt over ignoring that information and it is easy to be wise after the event.' The policeman had flushed at the implied rebuke. 'Two nights ago one of the children at the orphanage woke up in the small hours of the morning and looked out of the dormitory window. She claimed to have seen a human figure prowling around the grounds but, as it was a dark night and she couldn't even say if the figure was male or female, we dismissed the story as childish imagination.'

'And because you dismissed it, six more people have died.' For the first time Eric Yeats looked up. 'So simple, isn't it, gentlemen? You substitute petrol for diesel fuel, introduce dynamite and they die; all of them. Alec Mason, Peter Fletcher, L'Eclus and Sylvia

Rheinhart, Straker and old Malcolm Starr. Six good friends gone in a single moment of time and now General Kirk tells me that those other deaths were murder as well.' He turned and stared at Marcus.

'Why, Levin? Why should anybody want to do these things? Is that single woman responsible or is the general right? Is some organization at work which hopes to destroy our whole Fellowship? Who have we harmed? What has caused such hatred against us?'

'Take it easy, Dr Yeats.' Marcus was studying the man's hands which had been shaking so badly that he now gripped the chair arms to control them. 'Slasher' Yeats had always been a jolly, extroverted man in the past. An after-dinner speaker, a presenter of prizes, the non-playing captain of a hospital rugger club. He had also earned his nickname by being one of the fastest and steadiest surgeons of his generation. Now he could hardly have signed his own name. 'They'll find that woman very soon and then we'll know the truth about everything.'

'You say take it easy. Eleven of us have been killed already and you can say that.' Yeats's lips were like worms crawling across his face. 'If it hadn't been for the firework party, every single member of the Fellowship would have been on that launch, gentlemen. Those of us who could spare the time decided to stay on, you see. The anniversary party was pretty dull for the kids and we intended to give them a really good one on November the fifth. Without that . . .' Yeats lowered his head, obviously ashamed of the tears in his eyes.

'Don't worry, Doctor. Anna Harb will be found before she can do any more harm.' Cameron opened a filing cabinet and produced a glass and a bottle of clear liquid. 'Police reinforcements are arriving from the mainland and troops are on their way. Now, please drink this. It's pure Skye whisky and there is nothing better for the nerves.'

'How long will it take to search the whole island, Chief Constable?' Kirk had stood up and was looking out of the window at the little sleepy town which was already swarming with reporters and morbid sightseers. Beyond it lay long ridges of hills and deep valleys, normally deserted except for sheep and wild goats, crags where eagles nested and caves that had never been explored. Now police and local volunteers were beating those hills for a phantom and before long troops and aircraft would join them. One woman against an army, but Kirk had never realized the emptiness of the Western Islands and he knew it might take a long time to find her. He also felt a slight twinge of guilt for his dislike of John Forest. The man had paid for his story and now lay in hospital, concussed by a piece of falling wreckage that had struck the ferry. The fellow had been correct when he described the difficulties involved and, one day, Kirk intended to apologize to him.

'God knows, General.' The laird was standing before a map on the wall. 'This island is thirty miles long and sixteen miles across at its broadest point. Since the First World War, the population has been steadily decreasing and we now number less than five thousand souls, most of them concentrated in and around Lochern.' His finger traced the outline of Bala which was rather like a thumbless hand with Lochern at the base of the palm and four promontories pointing out into the Atlantic.

'Empty crofts, gentlemen, deserted farm buildings and many, many caves. In the summer parties of climbers and hill walkers often arrive without tents or hotel bookings because there is so much free accommodation for them. Only last year our local traders' association petitioned the council to tear the roofs from all disused buildings as they were ruining business.' Cameron turned to the bowed figure on the chair. The whisky had given Yeats a trace of colour but his eyes still showed strain and utter misery.

'Inver House was almost a ruin when your Fellowship purchased it seven years ago, Doctor, and there are five deserted houses on the peninsula where it is situated. You have my promise that Anna Harb will be found, but it may take some time.'

'But when you find her, will the danger have passed, Chief Constable?' Marcus had derided Kirk's theory that there was a conspiracy at work against the Van Traylen Fellowship, but recent events were changing his mind. He had seen the woman, he had looked into her face. He knew she was insane and he could easily imagine her making a further attack on her child or on individual members of the Fellowship who she believed had stolen Mary from her. She might have used a knife, or a gun, or her bare hands, but this cold-blooded planning did not fit her personality at all.

'How can we be sure that Harb is working alone on the island, or that she was responsible for the sabotage of the launch? The use of dynamite and the substitution of petrol for diesel oil implies a specialized knowledge which she probably did not possess.'

'Ah, but she did, Sir Marcus.' Inspector Grant took a folder from a filing cabinet. 'This is the Yard's dossier on Harb. Until recently it was incomplete because, during the years '60 and '61 she was out of the country and lived with this man.' He handed Kirk and Marcus two photostat copies of a report in French. 'The Sûreté have now filled in the blanks for us and I think you may have heard of him, General.'

'Yes, I knew him . . . knew of him, that is.' Kirk was studying a photograph clipped to the top of the sheet. A good face, as far as it went, he thought. A broad forehead, a strong nose and a pair of clear, smiling eyes. The trouble was that it did not go far enough. The lower lip ran straight down to join the neck almost without the dignity of a chin and the general effect was of a classical sculpture of which the artist had grown bored and left unfinished.

'Robert Nord. Resistance hero known by the code name of "The Sparrow",' Kirk translated. 'Member of a group which attacked and destroyed a German troop train outside Lille, January '43. Led the attack on the Villavignette radio station in September of the same year. Between January '44 and the end of hostilities is claimed to have destroyed a minimum of eighteen military vehicles. Granted membership of the Legion of Honour, June '45.

'So much for the hero.' Kirk frowned as he read on down the close typing. The sparrow had had its flight, but it couldn't settle down in captivity. The years of peace showed convictions for fraud, theft and malicious wounding. Then, when the Muslim rebellion in Africa turned to civil war, M. Nord had found his vocation again as a member of the O.A.S., the Secret Army Organization, and his *plastiques* had roared in the streets of Algiers and Oran. Finally had come his last blow. To bring the war home to the people of France itself, a band of saboteurs had landed at Marseilles and

placed time-bombs in a petrol refinery. Eight men, a woman and a
child had died in the ensuing explosion and their murderers soon
followed them. On December 8th, 1961, a guillotine had neatly
removed Nord's head.

'Yes, Mark,' Kirk said as he handed the sheet back to the inspector. 'If Harb was this joker's girl friend, she would have known
how to blow up that launch all right.'

'But I still don't see the motive.' Marcus was staring at the photograph as if Nord's chinless face fascinated him. 'From what I
saw and from Haynes's notes, we know that the woman has an
obsessive hatred towards her daughter and feels that the Fellowship stole Mary from her. We also know that she was on drugs and
such people can often be used as tools by their suppliers. But I just
cannot believe that she sabotaged the launch single-handed.'

'It does sound improbable, Sir Marcus.' The Chief Constable
nodded. 'All the same, Harb's fingerprints were found in that Dormobile which was hired in London and we know she must be on
Bala. By noon tomorrow I shall have over a thousand troops comb-
ing the island and they are bound to find her in time. When they
do, she will be made to talk and then we shall know the truth.

'Excuse me, though.' The phone rang and he stomped across
to his desk. 'Yes, this is the Chief Constable speaking. Oh, good
afternoon, Mrs Alison. What is that? Two hours ago and you say
that you've searched the buildings and the grounds thoroughly?' A
dark shadow crept across the leathery skin as he listened.

'Now, madam, I am quite sure there is no need for anxiety, but
please hold the line for a moment.' He cupped a hand over the
mouthpiece and looked at Grant.

'I told you to have a man stationed inside the orphanage and to
seal off the whole area, Inspector. Has that been done?'

'No, sir, it has not.' Once again the policeman bridled at the
implied rebuke. 'Mrs Alison herself, the matron, refused to let me
put a constable inside the grounds because she said it might distress the children who are being kept in ignorance of the events.

'As for sealing off the entire area, I am not a magician, Chief
Constable.' He crossed over to the map and pointed at the most
northerly peninsula. 'Two men, one of them a dog handler, have

been told to patrol the orphanage walls during the hours of darkness and a road block has been set up here. Counting police reinforcements and local volunteers I have less than sixty men at my disposal and you have ordered me to search the entire island. The Morfar peninsula is seven miles long, all of it difficult country with plenty of cover. There is a party of volunteers with binoculars on Ben Tarbert, there is the road block, but with respect, sir, I can't do more till the troops get here.'

'All right, Inspector.' Cameron lifted the telephone. 'Mrs Alison, as I have said, I am sure that there is no need to worry. The little boy is playing a game with you and will be hiding somewhere. Boys do that; I've got three of my own. He'll come out as soon as he is hungry and my advice is that you give the dinner gong an extra loud bang. All the same, I'd better have his description, just in case.' He picked up a pencil and a memo pad.

'Sidney Molson . . . seven years and one month old . . . tall for his age and fair-haired . . . wears a dental brace. You missed him approximately two hours ago.

'Thank you, Mrs Alison. We have a patrol outside the orphanage so I'm quite sure Sidney is somewhere in the grounds and safe and sound. For the time being keep all the children together and I'll be with you as soon as possible.' The Chief Constable spoke with the false confidence of a frightened man and his knuckles were dead white as he replaced the instrument.

'You've nothing to reproach yourself for, Inspector Grant. If anything has happened to that child, the blame will be mine. I should have told you to concentrate every man you've got on Morfar and leave the rest of the island till the soldiers arrive.' He took his coat from a rack and stood staring at them in turn; Kirk and Marcus and the naval officer, Grant and Yeats and finally back to Kirk.

'You all heard that, gentlemen,' he said. 'Another of 'em. A little boy called Sidney Molson missing since eleven o'clock. Obviously playing a joke and hiding somewhere . . . children do . . . bound to turn up before we get there.' There was a rumble of heavy vehicles and he crossed to the window to watch a convoy of army lorries move into the square.

'Thank God those chaps are here at last. We'll find her soon, General. A thousand men, they promised me. Dogs and helicopters and track-laying vehicles too. All that against one woman.' Cameron pulled on his coat and his voice was barely audible above the roar of the convoy.

'I've lived on Bala most of my life, gentlemen. Family been here for over twenty generations. Usually felt it was a friendly island; home, warmth, security. Now, I'm not sure . . . Not sure about anything any more.' As he put on his hat, Marcus saw that the laird's hands were shaking as badly as Yeats's had done.

'Always thought of the Devil as male . . . now . . . perhaps a woman.'

Chapter Eleven

THE MAJORITY of 'B' Company were enjoying themselves because they were keen. 'A good lively bunch, apart from a small minority,' the adjutant had remarked to the colonel only a week ago. 'If it wasn't for a couple of shirkers, my lot would be the best in the brigade,' Lieutenant Frisby frequently boasted in the Mess. 'Not a bad mob as peacetime soldiers go,' Regimental Serjeant Major Hiscock had begrudgingly admitted. 'Though there are two idle bastards I'd like to see in the glass-house.'

'B' Company had arrived on Bala in a blaze of publicity which pleased them greatly. Cameras had whirred and flashed as they landed at the quay. Children and girls had waved and cheered their entrance into Lochern as if they were the vanguard of some liberating army, and they had seen at least a dozen newspapermen making notes of their progress. The majority were also serious and public-spirited men, with a high regard for their calling and responsibilities. Somewhere on the island a dangerous maniac was lurking and it was up to them to discover her hiding place. They had the best officers, the best equipment, the best *esprit de corps* in the British army and it was they who would find Anna Harb. The majority were only too pleased to be scouring the hillsides and they worked with a will, toiling up scree and down valley and only pausing to lift their walkie-talkies and communicate with the helicopter which hovered overhead.

'Ker-ist, Jesus unprintable Ker-ist.' As one man the tiny minority halted, scanned the horizons to see if they could be observed and lowered themselves on to a shelf of dry heather. '"Join the modern army, eh?"' Private Smith remarked to Private Hutchinson. '"Mechanization is today's key word," they keep repeating like a cage of bloody parrots.' He pulled out a crumpled packet of cigarettes. 'I've just about had a bellyfull of this caper, Hutch. Me feet ache, I'm dead beat and I think I broke a rib, maybe two, when I fell over that sodding boulder just now.'

'You can count me in on sodding, Jack.' Hutchinson stared gloomily up at the face of Ben Lind, towering a thousand feet above them. Their company was spread out along its five-mile slopes and on either side they could see the brightly coloured anoraks of the other teams well in advance of them and gaining steadily.

'Ta, Jack.' He accepted a light and inhaled greedily. To their right, the peninsula curved out into the Atlantic and, through a gap in the crags, they could just make out the orphanage buildings in the far distance, while to the south and east, the mainland hills stretched away in long purple lines. The whole scene was strikingly lovely, but the only beauty Hutchinson appreciated was the female form which may not always be divine, whatever poets say.

'Rover Dog Party, where are you?' The intercom crackled and they saw the helicopter come wheeling over the mountain. 'You should be halfway up the ridge by now and in plain sight. Report at once, Rover Dog.'

'Rover Dog answering, sir.' Smith stood up hurriedly. The wind had been blowing towards the aircraft and they had not heard its approach.

'We are at the foot of a vertical cliff face, sir, which looks dangerous, and there appears to be no means of ascending it. I submit that it would be best for us to find a more easy way round across the moor.' He looked longingly at the level route behind them.

'You will do nothing of the sort, Private Smith.' Lieutenant Frisby's voice was a mixture of despair and cold fury. 'All the other teams are finding a way up and you must use your initiative. The whole point of the operation is that we keep in line together.' He paused, obviously studying the terrain.

'Yes, I can see you, Rover Dog. Now, look to your right. Can you make out a rock pinnacle shaped rather like a man's head?'

'Yes, sir, but I still don't think that . . .'

'Then don't think, Smith; climb.' Frisby had been following the police procedure of containing vice in one area when he placed Hutchinson and Smith together and already he regretted the decision. 'From up here I can see that beyond that pinnacle there is a perfectly easy gully leading to the summit. I want to have you both on the top within an hour. Now get going, Rover Dog. Over and out.' The set cut off and the helicopter rattled away to encourage the other teams. Smith and Hutchinson threw away their cigarettes and plodded on across the wilderness of boulders that led to the base of the cliff.

'Seems all wrong somehow, Jack; hundreds of men hunting one poor woman.' Hutchinson was slightly ahead, toiling up the first of the scree shoots which filled the gorge. 'Unsportin' like.'

'Don't be so bloody silly, Hutch.' Smith scowled at two ravens circling overhead who now and again croaked hoarsely, as if mocking their slow progress. 'This thing we're after ain't a woman. Remember the pictures of 'er, remember all the geezers she's done in already, remember that loonies have twice the strength of normal people like you and me. I just 'ope we don't catch up with the bitch. Job for the police this should have been. And if they had to get troops to do their dirty work, they should at least 'ave armed us. "No rifles, lads," said the bleeding R.S.M. "You're 'ere to arrest a demented maniac, not fight a war."' A jagged rock wall barred their progress, the helicopter was a good mile away and he came to a halt and pointed up at two tiny figures scrambling towards the summit like apes. 'Look at those stupid sods. Must be Corporal Jones and old Wiggy Bennet. They'll get busted hearts running up like that.'

'Jolly good show, Hunting Dog. You're making excellent time.' A cheery voice rang out from the radio. 'Be sure to keep your eyes skinned for caves when you start down the other side, Hunting

Dog. It seems possible that the woman may be hiding out some-where on the lower slopes.

'Well done you too, Boxer Dog. Almost to the top, eh, and you had by far the stiffest pull. We'll have you in the Olympic team one day.

'What the hell . . . ? Rover Dog!' The aircraft had turned towards Hutchinson and Smith and all good humour left Frisby's voice. 'Why are you loitering there, Rover Dog? Get on and catch up with the others immediately. Do you hear me, Rover Dog?'

'Receiving you loud and clear, sir. I have merely halted to perform a natural function.' To prove the point, Smith turned and urinated down the hillside. 'Be up to the top in a brace of shakes, sir.'

'You had better be, unless you want me to deal with you.' A voice with a snap and a bark and a growl in it took over from the lieutenant. 'I know you, Private Smith. I know you too, Hutchin-son. I dislike both of you. It will give me great pleasure to punish you. Good God, men, don't you realize the situation. That woman has to be found. She is an insane killer and she probably has a child with her. She may be attacking that child while you stand there loafing. Get up the mountain and be quick about it.'

'We'll do our 'uman best, sir. Can't say no more than that.' Smith grinned, but Hutchinson was already scrambling up the slab.

'Come on, Jack. That was the R.S.M. and I'm in his bad books already. Don't make it worse for me.' That was putting things very mildly. The unit had recently been stationed near a large public school and a rugger match had been arranged between an army side and its first fifteen. The game had been close and exciting and the troops had cheered their team enthusiastically while the boys kept up monotonous bird-like chants of 'School-School . . . Well played, School . . . Heel, School . . . Come on, School.' There had been an embarrassed silence however after Regimental Serjeant Major Hiscock had been brought crashing to earth and Hutch's voice had roared across the field, 'Gouge him, School . . . Bite him, School . . . kick the rotten bastard in the teeth, School.'

'All right, mate, but remember I've got the radio to hump.' Smith fingered the harness of the walkie-talkie. 'Rot the man who first invented transistors. If this had been a valve set we could have broken it, accidentally like, and the sods couldn't have bothered us.' He shrugged his shoulders, wiped his sweating forehead and followed his companion up the mountain.

It took them a long time to reach the top of the ridge, and when they finally got there dusk had started to close in and mist was drifting up from the sea. There had been no sign of the helicopter for a good half hour and none of the other parties were in sight. The climb had been hot in the sunlight, but now the sun had gone down they both felt the sudden cold. Below them the other side of the mountain appeared to stretch endlessly away through scree and boulders and isolated crags, and the moor below it looked dead and hostile.

'I don't like this, Hutch.' Smith had been born and lived most of his life in a crowded tenement and the desolation of the place worried him. 'I know there are two of us, but I hope to hell we don't catch up with that woman. Some of the lads might have waited for us if they'd had any decency. No joke going down there in the dark either. All we've got is a torch and they should've given us ropes and pulleys and special equipment.'

'Still we gotta get down, Jack.' Hutchinson consulted his watch. 'We was told to rendezvous at the orphanage gates by sixteen thirty hours and time's getting on. They won't make the trucks wait for us . . . not for us they won't, and we'll have to slog all the way back to camp.' He glanced towards a cluster of lights across the moor and then opened his map.

'That must be the orphanage straight ahead, but there's no point in trying to get there on time. What we'd best do is to cut over to the left. The road's down there and we may be able to intercept the convoy. The captain'll have kittens at first, but when you see the lorries sling your arm around me shoulders, limp like buggery and play up that fall you had earlier on.'

'That's the ticket.' The range sloped far less steeply to the left and Smith's spirits returned. '"Make room for a wounded hero, mate. Give this poor man a hand up into the lorry, Corporal."'

'Let's get going before the fog cuts us off, Hutch. I seem to remember there was a lighthouse near the road. They'll probably start letting off a signal gun if it gets really thick.'

They hurried quickly down the hillside, but the mist was far quicker. It rose in thick grey spirals, filling every gully and crevice, and as dusk fell their only sense of direction came from the sloping terrain and the lighthouse. Smith had been right about the signal gun and every five minutes the rocks echoed dully with the distant explosions. As the angle of the mountain turned, however, the echoes appeared as real as the original detonations and the gun became a worthless guide.

'Blimey, Jack, this is no fun at all.' Hutchinson had stumbled into a patch of marsh and was up to his knees in slime. 'It's getting darker and darker every minute. Let's have a squint at the compass. I haven't a clue which way the road is.'

'Compass? But I gave it to you, mate. Don't you remember when we stopped for a smoke at the foot of that bleeding cliff?'

'Yers, you're right at that. I must have left it there after Frisby bawled us out.'

'Well, we'll just have to take pot luck then.' Smith suddenly stiffened and pointed uphill. 'Do you hear something, Hutch? Something moving above us?'

'I can and all. I can smell it too.' He gripped his friend's arm as he heard a tinkle of scree and smelt a rich, salty odour drifting down through the mist. 'That maniac's bound to be armed, Jack, and she could come creeping up behind us in this fog. Let's get on down and keep close together all the way.'

'No, wait a minute.' Smith was no hero, but he was not quite as abject as his friend. 'I think I can recognize that stench.' He picked up a stone and flung it into the mist. There was bellow of animal rage as the lucky shot found its target, and a big horned body hurtled past them and went clattering down the hillside.

'Just a bleedin' goat, Hutch. My old man used to keep a couple of the perishers in the back yard when we was kids.' He chuckled. 'Bit of luck for us too. I've heard that the brutes have regular paths to their drinking places. All we have to do is to follow him down, find a stream and that's bound to lead us to the coast road.'

'Okay, Jack, but for Gawd's sake let's keep close together.' Hutchinson staggered after him down the narrow goat track. It ran diagonally across the mountain, through damp gullies and over isolated cliff faces which made them crawl on their knees at times, while at every minute the mist and darkness grew thicker. Now and again, Hutchinson would turn and look anxiously around him, imagining that every boulder, every crevice, every rock wall screened a crazed, inhuman figure about to rush out at him through the gloom.

'Well, where's your blasted stream, Jack?' The track had finally petered out at the foot of the hillside and they had been tramping across level ground for the past ten minutes. 'I can't hear any running water.'

'Neither can I, but the road's bound to be somewhere ahead of us. It's gotta be.' Smith spoke loudly to reassure himself. 'Come on, Hutch, we can't be far off now.'

'I hope you're right, mate. Blimey I hope you are right!' Hutchinson plodded forward after him. There was no sense of gravity to help them now and soon the going became difficult again as the firm heather changed to peat hags and ridges of rotting vegetation, some so slippery that they had to be taken at a run. More often than not, one of them would fall and lie gasping in the sodden valleys, while at times the stuff was so soft that they had to wade through it up to their knees and their hands would bring huge armfuls tumbling down on top of them.

'Hutch! Where are you, Hutch?' Smith had made the quicker progress and he stopped on top of a ridge and screened his eyes against the fog. He knew that his friend could not be far behind, but could see no sign of him. 'Yell out and let me know where you are. I can't see a blasted thing.'

'I'm here, Jack, down here.' Hutchinson's voice was almost a sob. 'Come back quick and bring the torch with you. I fell just now and my hands went right through the bloody peat. I grabbed hold of something, Jack, and I think it may be . . .'

'Coming, Hutch.' Smith came running and stumbling across the ridges to where his friend was crouched on his knees. He could hear Hutchinson sobbing openly as he slid down beside him, and as he switched on the torch he understood why. A human face was staring out at them from the brown peat.

Chapter Twelve

'THAT WAS Sidney Molson, gentlemen.' The island possessed no proper morgue, only an out-house built on to the Cottage Hospital, and Grace Alison stood blinking in the sunlight as Inspector Grant closed the door behind her.

'He had been tortured, hadn't he? Killed slowly for pleasure.' Mrs Alison, the orphanage matron, a short capable woman who would normally appear bustling and cheerful, was a kindly disciplinarian who could run the lives of a large group of children and never reveal her own feelings. Now she looked like someone who had physically recovered from a long illness and, in the process, discovered that life had no meaning at all.

'Sidney was such a nice little boy, General. Always so friendly and cheerful, always affectionate, and yet this happened to him. To die like that, to be buried in the peat less than a mile away from our own grounds.' She allowed Kirk to take her arm and lead her into the hospital and to the almoner's office. 'How many wounds were there, General? What have we done to cause this hatred? When did it all start?'

'Sidney had been stabbed thirty-two times, Mrs Alison.' Kirk knew that she was the kind of woman who had to be told the truth, but he winced inwardly as he remembered his first sight of Sidney Molson. The little body had been lifted down from an army truck and it was naked and stained brown by the peat which had been its shroud. At a brief glance the boy looked unmarked and peaceful, almost as if he were sleeping, then they had wiped away the stains and it was possible to see the marks of a thin knife that had run him through and through as though he were a pin cushion. The coroner and Marcus had agreed that only three of them could have caused death and the others were clearly intended for the infliction of pain.

'It doesn't do to dwell on these things, Mrs Alison, and very soon the woman is bound to be found.' He watched Cameron pour out a cup of tea and saw her take it in a hand that did not tremble at all. 'The Chief Constable has ample men at his disposal at last and it is just a question of time.' Kirk spoke to reassure himself, but through the window the shadows of the lowering hills mocked him. He had the sudden and unpleasant feeling that Anna Harb was not a creature of the world at all, but a demon and the mountains were allies who would hide her for ever.

'It will take a specialist in morbid psychology to understand Harb's motives, but for the moment may I ask you one or two questions?'

'If you wish, General, though I have told the Inspector all I know. We missed Sidney shortly after eleven o'clock. We have no idea how or why he left the grounds of the house.' Grace Alison sipped at the tea, holding the cup in a hand which still remained quite steady, though her face was tortured.

'I know that, madam. Inspector Grant has already shown me your evidence.' Kirk gave the policeman a brief nod.

'But it is the background of the Fellowship itself I would like to hear about. I have always understood that it is very difficult to adopt children these days, that there is a waiting list for all except the abnormal, and to collect so many normal and healthy children and place them in a private home would be very difficult indeed. How did your society go about it?'

'General Kirk, I really do not see the point in such a question. Mrs Alison is naturally distressed and she has told us all we need to know for the time being.' Cameron broke in angrily, but the woman waved aside the interruption.

'No, I would like to reply to the General's question, though I fancy he already knows the answer.' Her voice had a ring of quiet authority as if she were calming a fractious child.

'You are quite right of course, General Kirk. Private families are clamouring to adopt children and it would have been impossible for us to fill our home in the normal manner. We had to go into the gutter for them.' She was looking at Marcus who stood rigidly by the far wall.

'Our charges are all normal, healthy children of high intelligence, Sir Marcus, but they have backgrounds which many people might find frightening—the offspring of criminals and the mentally unstable. You all know what Anna Harb is, while Sidney Molson's parents both committed suicide by slashing their wrists, and the child witnessed it. Does that answer your question, General?'

'Yes, madam, it does.' Kirk stared gloomily out of the window, the woman took another sip from her cup, Cameron and the police inspector were considering the terrain of the island—the areas that had been searched, those which remained, the few possible hiding places that were left for Anna Harb—and for a moment there was silence. Marcus was thinking about Peter Haynes.

For Haynes should have realized what caused Mary Valley's night terrors; not hereditary insanity, not any racial memories of the past, but something much simpler. An insane mother who not only dabbled in the occult but had tried to give her daughter clairvoyant powers too. What had been done to that little girl before she was removed from Harb's care? What mental and physical suffering had been inflicted during her training? Above all, what was significant about those patterned wounds on Sidney Molson's body? Though he was a scientist and normally rejected the supernatural as unproven, Marcus felt that they should tell him something which was without any logical basis.

'Now, General, may we know the reason for your rather extraordinary line of questioning?' Without any embarrassment the Chief Constable had raised a hip flask to his lips and knocked back a stiff peg of whisky.

'We are hunting a murderess who is known to have an insane hatred of not only her own daughter, but the whole of the Van Traylen Fellowship which she believes stole the child from her. All we have to do is to find that woman and everything else is unimportant.'

'You are probably right.' Normally Kirk would have snapped back at the rebuke, but he was too tired and bewildered to feel any resentment. 'All the same, I feel sure that Anna Harb cannot be the only force at work. It is inconceivable that one woman could have accomplished so much or remained undetected over such a long period.' He kept glancing at his companions in turn as he tried to explain his theory, and every word caused him acute embarrassment because he knew it was untenable. That Anna Harb was not the only parent who felt that her child had been stolen from her and turned against her to become a soul that should not have been born. That a group of crazy men and women were engaged in a war against the Fellowship; plotting and watching and waiting for the opportunity to strike and destroy every member of the society which Helen Van Traylen had founded for the benefit of young and old alike. That the war would continue long after Anna Harb was found. That some of these people could be on the island now, hidden amongst the crowds of sightseers which had filled the ferry boats at every recent sailing.

'Tell me something, Sir Marcus.' Mrs Alison had obviously not been listening to Kirk but had stared at Marcus all the time he was speaking. 'You are a doctor and you examined the little boy's body. Were the wounds simply delivered out of wanton cruelty, or was there a pattern to them?'

'There was a pattern, I'm afraid.' As he answered, that broken, tortured body was clear behind Marcus's eyes. Wanton stabs and slashes, three deep wounds, any one of which would have caused death, but there had also been holes through each foot and palm, a gash in the side and a criss-cross of scratches on the forehead which might have been caused by thorns. 'You think that Sidney's murder may have been a ritual killing, Mrs Alison?'

'I think nothing, Sir Marcus.' She took off her glasses and polished them with a handkerchief. Without them her eyes were very bright and intelligent, though full of suffering.

'All I know is that I am suddenly very frightened because I have always considered the possibility of a force of pure evil and I am now sure that it exists.'

'Madam, General Kirk, Sir Marcus, please let us try to keep a sense of perspective.' Good, pious materialism thundered from the inspector's lips. 'There is no ten-headed devil walking those hills, but a criminal lunatic who will be under lock and key at any moment.

'And that could very well tell us that she already is.' An intercom whirred on the desk and he hurried over to answer it.

'Inspector Grant here.' He pressed a switch and a shrill, anxious, but also demanding voice came through the loudspeaker.

'Is Mrs Alison there? I want Mrs Alison? We all want her . . . Tell her to come home now . . . at once,' said the voice which Marcus recognized as Mary Valley's.

Chapter Thirteen

MORE troops had landed during the night and a convoy was driving into Lochern as they left the town. Police and soldiers on motor bicycles kept roaring past them and once they had to give way to a party of farmers mounted on shaggy Highland ponies. They also knew that lookouts were stationed on every major peak. Bala was a small island and yard by yard it was being combed to find a single woman. So far the Dormobile was the only proof of her existence.

'Why can't he drive faster?' The police car was crawling along the narrow road held back by Cameron's aged Morris and Mrs Alison turned to Kirk and Marcus on the seat behind her. 'I know they must be safe, that the grounds are cordoned off, but after hearing that child on the telephone . . .'

'Don't worry, dear lady.' Kirk gave a reassuring smile. Mary Valley had not sounded frightened or anxious on the telephone, but demanding. 'Come back . . . We need you . . . Now.' She might have been a domineering employer speaking to a servant.

'Some terrible things have happened, but I am convinced the danger is over, Mrs Alison. The orphanage is cordoned off, as you say, and the woman is bound to be found at any moment. Aren't I right, Constable?'

'Maybe, General.' The driver lifted a gloved hand and pointed out to sea. A drifter was lying hove to on the swell, and they could see a group of men on her bridge scanning the coastline through binoculars and telescopes. 'They're doing all they can, but this is a wild country. I mind that two winters back a party of boy scouts were lost on the Blyven Range over yonder.' His hand pointed inland at a line of jagged crags to the left and Marcus fancied he could see a group of figures toiling up the nearest ridge. 'For a full week we searched for the bairns, and when we found them, in a cave where they'd been sheltering, the poor wee souls had been dead for three days, frozen solid. Aye, a wild, sad island is Bala. They say that it is lonely and likes to hide things and keep them to itself.' The road had turned seaward towards a wide, sandy cove and he pointed again. 'That is Spaniards' Bay and an Armada ship is down there somewhere. She is supposed to have foundered while sheltering from a gale. The *Santa Pilar* her name was, and the story went that she carried gold and silver coin to pay the whole army in Flanders. Maybe that was just wishful thinking, but she is certainly said to have sunk there and the old laird, the Chief Constable's father, wellnigh beggared the family sending divers down to look for her. The strange thing is that, though the ocean bed is clear rock with no sludge at all, they didn't come up with so much as a single piece of timber.

'Perhaps I shouldn't be saying this, Mrs Alison, but even after what she's done I can't help feeling sorry for that poor demented creature if she's hiding out on our hills. The tourists come and admire them from motor cars, climbers and hikers rave over them, but most of the island folk hate every crag and glen of the old devils.'

'I think I can understand what you mean.' Marcus always felt vaguely ill-at-ease and excited amongst hills and there was something both sad and menacing about these. To the south, the blue Cuillins of Skye dominated the horizon, and behind him the mainland peaks stretched away towards the north. They looked quite different to the bleak mountains of Bala. The land which the gods had forgotten, the early Norse explorers had called the island; a place which likes to hide things and keep them to itself. Like the driver, Marcus also felt sympathy for Anna Harb. A murderess, a maniac bent on some horrible war of revenge and destruction, but also pathetic; still a human being with the forces of both man and nature pitted against her. He could not accept Kirk's theories that Anna Harb had accomplices and he had given up trying to form a theory for himself. In his own mind he was quite sure she was completely alone.

'You'd know it better, if you stayed on Bala for a year, sir.' The driver drew up in a passing place to allow a lorry filled with marine commandos to thunder by. 'Each year at the opening of the games, the laird makes the same speech about it being the home which we will always come back to, but I think he's trying to convince himself. Why, there were twenty thousand souls on the island before the first war and less than five thousand at the last census.' He let in the clutch, nodding towards a ruined farm house by the roadside. A stunted tree grew through its broken roof and creepers covered the walls, giving it the appearance of a yew hedge which had been trained and moulded for centuries in an English park.

'Do you mind what happened when they started the ferry service, Mrs Alison?' The driver was bored by crawling behind Cameron and he obviously liked the sound of his own voice. 'In the old days, John Gordon's motor boat was the only link we had with the outside world, but then the railway built the jetty at Lochern and advertised the car ferries. They thought they would encourage the tourist trade and bring the people back to the island. But exactly the opposite happened and they've been losing money ever since. When the first steamer tied up, there were half a dozen families waiting to go back on her. They'd finally been given the chance to get their furniture over to the mainland. I'll be off myself, as soon as my old mother has passed away, gentlemen. Three of the family are in Canada already and they say that there's grand openings for a man over there.'

'They must find her soon.' Kirk was watching a naval helicopter circling low down over the moor. 'The army and the navy and the marines. Every modern aid against a single woman. She can't hide out for much longer.'

'My guess is that they'll never find her, General.' Kirk had spoken to Marcus but it was the driver who answered. 'It's my belief that the poor, crazed creature is dead already and the earth has taken her. She buried the little boy in the peat on Sperry Wastes, and between the wastes and Ben Lind there are bogs which could swallow a battleship. No, Anna Harb won't trouble you any more, Mrs Alison. She'd be deep under the ground and you can stop worrying.

'Ah, get on, your lordship, please get on.' Cameron's car had stopped at a check point controlled by soldiers and was now lurching up a slope that led away from the sea. 'The laird's done a hundred and fifty thousand miles in that old Morris and he boasts that he only gets it serviced every twelvemonth. She's going to let him down badly one of these days.

'That's Inver House over there, gentlemen.' As the car finally topped the slope they could see a rectangle of buildings surrounded by a stone wall. There was a green field beyond them contrasting vividly with the bracken and heather, and beyond the grass basalt cliffs fell straight down into the sea.

'Well, everything appears to be under control, Mrs Alison.' One of the policemen on duty before the gate held open the car doors and Cameron came grinning towards them. 'Everybody all present and accounted for, but Serjeant Mackay here tells me that Lord Fawnlee still refuses to let him station men inside the grounds. Most unwise that; asking for trouble in my opinion.'

'Michael Fawnlee knows what he is doing, Chief Constable.' With Cameron's assurance that all was well, some of the strain had left her face. 'We don't want the children to know what is happening, as I told you. We are most grateful for your protection, but the presence of strangers in the grounds would be bound to show them that something is wrong. Now, if you'll excuse me, I must go and see why Mary telephoned.' Mrs Alison turned and hurried off through the gates.

'Poor, demented fools.' Cameron snorted. 'They don't seem to realize that without full co-operation we can't give them any proper protection at all. Why don't you and Sir Marcus go in and try to put some sense into 'em, General? They might listen to strangers. Probably think I'm just an officious old fool.

'And what the hell are those young hooligans doing here, Serjeant Mackay?' A hundred yards away a group of thirty or more teenagers were sprawled out on the heather watching the gate with morbid fascination. 'I gave orders that this area was to be cleared and it's still crawling with Glasgow keelies. Nobody appears to pay the slightest attention to me, man. Do I have to see to everything personally?

'You boys, clear off immediately. Get back to the road and out of here, do you hear me? I am the Chief Constable of the island and I have forbidden civilians to come past that check point.' The laird brandished his walking stick and marched purposefully over the moor as if preparing for the charge at Culloden.

'A sad place with a very sad history, Mark.' Kirk had been reading a local guide book and he looked interestedly around the quadrangle as they followed Mrs Alison through the gate. Inver House had been a Norman castle once, and before that a Viking fort. Wotan had been worshipped there and Christian missionaries hurled head first from the cliffs. Then Celt and Viking had intermarried, producing families which were often a strange mixture of dark-and fair-haired children, and the centuries had passed through a series of petty wars and forays. At the foot of the main building it was still possible to see the foundations of the medieval keep and Kirk had read that two of the island's hereditary chieftains had been beheaded in its main hall. But not only Scotsmen had suffered at Inver House. Another Armada ship, a Portuguese galleas, sheltered in the bay and her crew had been welcomed ashore and then stripped naked by the local inhabitants and turned out to starve on the hills. Charles Edward Stuart was said to have slept the night there during his flight from Skye, and a supposedly tear-stained pillow was lodged in an Edinburgh museum as proof. After the depopulation of the Highlands, the building had remained an empty shell till a Victorian speculator built the present structure: a huge pile of Highland baronial architecture, with mock towers and battlements resembling Glamis, heraldic beasts mounted around the walls and two cannon stationed before the main entrance. The speculator had intended to use it as an hotel, but he had died bankrupt with his work unfinished and the structure had slowly decayed; a shelter for sheep and a home for ravens. A few more decades would have revealed a complete ruin, but seven years ago the Van Traylen Fellowship had come on the scene.

'They've spent a devil of a lot of money on it, Charles.' Marcus noted the freshly painted stonework, the green lawn, the swimming pool, and line of children's slides and swings. It really did look as if the old house might have a purpose at last, but he supposed that that was over. Ten of the Van Traylen guardians were dead and the Fellowship was bound to break up. Then the children would be scattered into other homes and institutions and Inver House left to moulder again.

'Auntie . . . Auntie Alison. You're back at last. We've been waiting so long for you.' Shrill cries broke into their thoughts and they saw a group of children come running into the quadrangle. Behind the children came Lord Fawnlee and a tall, grey-haired woman they had not met before. The thing which astonished Kirk and Marcus was that all of them were smiling and laughing.

'Come with us, Auntie.' Mary Valley and another little girl clutched Grace Alison's arms. 'We've been making the guy for the party tonight and we want to show it to you.'

'And I want to see it, my dears, but the party won't be tonight, I'm afraid. I know it is November the fifth, but we'll have to put it off for just a few days.' Mrs Alison looked helplessly at Fawnlee for support, but he shook his head and smiled.

'No, Grace, we are not going to put it off. We are going to have our party on the proper date and it will be the best one we have ever had.' His eyes glistened with anticipation. 'Isn't that so, boys and girls?'

'Yes, yes, Uncle Michael.' The children clustered around them, tugging at their clothes and jumping up and down. 'The boys are bringing driftwood up from the beach for the bonfire and you must come and help us finish the clothes for the guy, Auntie.'

'Go with them, Grace.' There was sudden authority in the old man's voice. 'While you were out, Laura here and Eric Yeats and I have been talking things over. We have decided that, though we may still be in danger, though evil forces are at work against us, everything must go on as usual. Helen, our founder, wants that, Grace, and we have always obeyed her, haven't we?' He watched Mrs Alison follow the children into the building and then turned and held out his hand.

'General Kirk . . . Sir Marcus Levin. I am delighted to welcome you to Inver House. May I present my friend and colleague Dr Laura Rose, our resident medical officer.'

'A great pleasure, gentlemen.' As the woman stepped forward, they saw that she bore a similar stunned expression to that of Grace Alison, but there was no fear or despair in it. She was like someone who had spent years, wearing out her brain to discover some obscure truth and had finally found it. 'May I say how much I enjoyed your paper on the Enterin 156 Virus, Sir Marcus?'

'Thank you, Doctor.' Her grip was warm and firm, but Marcus felt a stab of cold as he looked into her eyes. Sidney Molson had been tortured to death, six human beings had died on the launch, somewhere among the hills a crazed woman might be hiding and waiting to strike again. But these children and old men and women laughed and smiled as if nothing had happened.

'Do you think that we are callous, Sir Marcus?' Fawnlee had noted his expression. 'Do you think we should weep and go into mourning and lock ourselves away in fear.' He smiled across towards the playground. No children were in sight, but they could hear laughter and the refrain of some nursery rhyme.

'You warned us, General Kirk. You said that evil forces were at work against us and you were right. But we are still not afraid, sir. We have been given grace, you see; the power of faith.' His left cheek twitched as he smiled and Marcus could see two completely separate individuals in the ravaged face: an old, broken man and the personality that had built a financial empire out of nothing.

'One woman . . . one evil creature has worked against us, but we do not fear her, gentlemen. We are not a religious body, but we do not mourn either, because we accept the resurrection of the soul. Everybody should do that if they hope to remain sane.' The words came dragging out like the tick of a clock that was running down. 'Our friends are not dead, they have merely walked out of one room and into another. You are an old man like me, General Kirk. Surely you believe that. You do not imagine your soul will die merely because the body rots.'

'Stop it, Michael.' The tall woman laid a hand on his arm. 'You are very tired indeed and you don't know what you are saying. I want you to go and lie down for an hour. Yes, that is an order, Michael.' She spoke as if to a child and, like a child, Fawnlee nodded and then walked wearily away.

'Please forgive him, General. I am not a psychologist but I think over-compensation is the term for my friend's condition. His mind is so stunned by what has happened that parts of it have rejected reality for the time being.' A breeze had started to blow and Laura Rose pushed back a strand of grey hair.

'Many of the others are like that too; even Eric Yeats, Sir Marcus. They are preserving their sanity by pretence. They refuse to admit that their friends are no longer with them, that the little boy was tortured to death. In my view it is a good thing that they do so.'

'Perhaps, Dr Rose, but I have something to ask you.' Kirk frowned as the children's laughter grew clearer on the breeze. 'The Chief Constable sent us here as emissaries. It is obvious that Anna Harb will be caught before long, probably within hours or even minutes, but surely it would be wise to let him station men inside the grounds. They would naturally be in plain clothes and the children could be told they were workmen.'

'There is no need for that, General Kirk. All the children will be kept in groups from now on and well protected.' She gave a slightly embarrassed smile and opened her handbag for him to see a small automatic lying between a purse and a powder compact. 'I have never used one of these things but the mechanism has been explained to me. Grace Alison has one too and we are not afraid of one woman.'

'I see.' There were two deep furrows below Kirk's mouth. Fawnlee was not the only person in a state of shock, he thought, and the notion of these two old ladies arming themselves with pistols gave him no comfort at all. Something hellish was at work against the society she served but, though Dr Rose appeared to speak sanely, she too had obviously been driven into a dream world.

But perhaps she was right in one thing. Perhaps Anna Harb really was working on her own and his long years in an intelligence service had made him think in terms of groups and unable to visualize such cunning and hatred in one individual. Perhaps the police were correct in still believing that the earlier deaths were accident or suicide. If they were discounted, there was nothing to support his theories about an organization and Anna Harb was a solitary figure, though an extremely sinister one. A woman with experience in sabotage, a known murderess, a maniac who had said that her child was an evil thing which had to be destroyed. She was also known to have practised black magic and Sidney Molson appeared to have been killed ritually. Could there be a history of Voodoo or some similar cult in her past?

'I said that I would like to show you around, General.' Laura Rose's voice interrupted his ponderings and Kirk nodded and followed her and Marcus across the square. The morning sky was clear and bright overhead, but a flock of gulls flying inland seemed to herald bad weather and he tightened his coat around him.

'Please do not let the children know that anything is wrong, gentlemen. They think that Sidney has gone away for a holiday and know nothing about the launch.' Dr Rose pointed across the playing field. The boys were hard at work building the bonfire and two adults were helping them: Eric Yeats and a man whose face Kirk recognized from the pages of the *Financial Times* and company prospectuses. Somehow the roles appeared to have been reversed and the old people were under orders from their charges. A dark bullet-headed boy of about nine was directing operations and giving his instructions in a high, excited voice.

'No, no, Uncle Eric, don't lay it sideways. The timbers must be stacked upright if the fire is to burn properly.'

Mary Valley really was a strange child, Kirk thought, remembering how she had tugged Mrs Alison's arm to take her off to help with the guy. Marcus's friend Haynes had said she was terrified of fire in any form, but Mary was clearly looking forward to this one. Child psychology was quite out of his province, though, and it was the psychology of Anna Harb that mattered at this moment. Kirk shivered and adjusted his muffler as he stared out to sea. The forecast of the birds was proving correct and a belt of cloud lay heavy over the horizon like a promise that the worst was yet to come.

Chapter Fourteen

'Please come home soon, Mark. I know I thought a change would do you good, but I've been so lonely without you. Goodbye, darling.' Tania Levin reluctantly replaced the telephone and crossed over to her bedroom window. Because it was Saturday, many people were holding their Guy Fawkes parties early and she could see a bonfire blazing in the next-door garden and rockets arching over the rooftops towards the setting sun.

It all sounds so crazy, she thought. Quite unbelievable. Nothing that Marcus had told her or what she had learned from the newspapers, radio or television made any sense at all. One single woman was supposed to have been responsible for everything; the earlier deaths, the well-planned destruction of the launch, and the ritual murder of the child. One woman was said to be holding Bala in a state of terror, and so far troops, police and local volunteers who knew the country had failed to find her though the island was small and sparsely populated.

'Completely incredible.' Tania looked into the dressing-table mirror and spoke aloud to her reflection in Russian. 'Anna Harb cannot be the only one. There must be an organization at work against the Fellowship. But why? For what reason?' Like Kirk, Tania had been trained in an intelligence service and automatically thought in terms of group action.

'Charles's theories are ridiculous, though. To imagine that a number of deranged parents wish to destroy the Fellowship because they consider it has stolen their children and alienated them. To suggest that the motive may be financial gain. That is slightly more feasible, but still very unlikely indeed. Who are these dispossessed heirs who employed an insane killer to reinstate them? If there was any truth in that, the police would have examined the beneficiaries and made them talk long ago.' Tania's knowledge of police interrogation came from men with more realistic views than those generally held in Western circles.

Yet there was a slight possibility that that theory might hold water, if the motives lay in the future and not in the past. Tania lit a cigarette and pondered on one of the maxims of her former chief, Gregor Petrov. 'Shear the sheep in public and the goats will not stray.' Was intimidation the key word, perhaps? A rich man or woman might think twice about willing a fortune to the Fellowship if he or she knew what happened to those that did.

'No, no, no.' Tania frowned at herself in the glass. 'That also is too incredible to be considered.' Yet the murders had taken place, the computer reading had been confirmed and some force, either

Anna Harb working on her own or an organization she belonged to, obviously intended to destroy the Van Traylen Fellowship.

'How would Gregor have tackled the problem?' She thought of him with deep affection. Petrov had retired long ago and now passed his time pottering about a flower garden in the Crimea. But for over a quarter of a century he had been a departmental boss of the Soviet Intelligence Service, surviving Stalin and Beria and weathering every political purge and change of leadership by a mixture of charm, cunning and utter ruthlessness. When a problem perplexed him, Petrov often quoted another maxim which he had stolen from Sherlock Holmes: 'Consider everything and discard everything which is not fact. What remains must be the truth, however unlikely it appears.'

'Well, the events that happened on Bala are facts,' Tania said to the mirror. 'The Dormobile was rented by Anna Harb, the launch did blow up, that poor little boy was tortured to death. But what about the earlier deaths? Mrs Van Traylen herself, the old colonel and the rest of them? The police had not considered the possibility of murder in a single instance and they are not facts. You would have dismissed them, wouldn't you, Gregor? You would have started to consider the case from the moment Mary Valley was admitted to Saint Bede's and examined by Peter Haynes.'

From down the street a clock started to strike the hour and she switched on her radio for the news from Station Charlotte. The announcer had a heavy cold and his voice sounded thick and slurred through the tiny loudspeaker of the transistor. She heard of the successful launching of an American moon probe, further financial squabbles in the Common Market, a cough and a splutter, an apology and . . . 'There is still no trace of Mrs Anna Harb who is wanted in connection with the murder of Dr Peter Haynes at Saint Bede's Hospital in West London last week. A police spokesman stated that the woman is almost certainly on the Island of Bala, though it appears doubtful whether she is still alive. Questions were asked about her in the House of Commons today. In reply to the Leader of the Opposition, Mr Ivor Mudd, the Home Secretary, stated amid shouts of "Resign" that well over a thousand men drawn from police reinforcements from the mainland

and members of the armed forces were engaged in searching the island for Mrs Harb. But their efforts were being severely hampered by crowds of morbid sightseers who had flocked on to Bala and acts of hooliganism were taking place there. Until the woman was apprehended, the ferry service from Torar to Lochern would be restricted to local inhabitants and persons on official business.

'The go-slow at Liverpool docks is now in its third week and . . .'

Over a thousand men! Tania turned off the set. It hardly seemed possible; men with helicopters and radios and dogs to help them. People with friends may remain undetected in cities for long periods, but surely not alone and in open country with that kind of force hunting them. Either the woman was being hidden by someone, or Marcus was correct in saying she was probably dead, lying broken in a crevice or swallowed by a bog.

Back to the beginning . . . back to Haynes. Tania watched another salvo of rockets soar into the darkening sky. For three years, Anna Harb had made no move against her child. It was only after Haynes came on the scene that Mary's troubles began.

Everything had pivoted on Haynes at first. He was the one person who credited the coach driver's story that a little girl had burned his face and caused the accident. Tania glanced at the glowing tip of her cigarette. Haynes had been so worried about Mary Valley's condition that he had risked infecting her with a dangerous culture so that she would have to be detained in hospital. He had also risked allowing Anna Harb, whom he knew to be a criminal lunatic, to visit the child and paid for it with his life.

Tania's hand fondled the bulge of her stomach. She was seven months pregnant and the thought of what happened in that gay, cosy room filled her with nausea. By all accounts, Harb had appeared quite normal when she arrived at Saint Bede's. What had caused the sudden change? What had been said or done to produce the maniac violence; the hatpin slashing out into Haynes's forehead; the child's screams as she was dragged to the well of the stairs; the woman raving just before Marcus reached them and the handbag swung out: 'The soul that should not have been born'?

Tania turned and gave a slightly nervous glance towards the

books beside her bed. She had been brought up as an enforced materialist, and since coming to England inquiry into the occult had fascinated her. The bedside lamp lit up the covers of *The Cult of the Werewolf*, *The Tibetan Book of the Dead* and *The Devil in Western Europe*. Anna Harb had practised as a clairvoyant and claimed to have the second sight; that was fact. She had tried to impart that power to her daughter; that was known from the magistrate's findings which had removed Mary from her care. Could that be a clue to the woman's motives, if not her whereabouts? Had Harb feared that Haynes had pried too deeply into Mary's mind and was about to reveal the things she had hidden there?

Perhaps the whereabouts too? Tania stubbed out the cigarette which had burned almost down to her fingers. People with secret beliefs and practices usually have special means of recognizing each other; by signs, by handshakes, by a certain way of speaking; even by an aura as sexual perverts are claimed to do.

It might be something like that. She glanced at a library book she had obtained that morning, *The Legacy of Bala*. It was mainly concerned with the island's scenery and natural history but a chapter was devoted to a folklore that went far back beyond Christian times to the old gods—Thor and Odin and Freyr. The author claimed that those deities had been secretly worshipped on Bala at least as recently as the turn of the century. Anna Harb was concerned with the occult. Was it possible she had arrived there alone but found co-religionists to shelter her?

'No, no, no, Comrade Valina.' Tania rapped the dressing-table and mimicked Gregor Petrov's gruff barks of annoyance. 'Facts, facts, facts, little Tania. In this department we do not deal with suppositions. Give me one definite fact or keep your mouth closed.'

But whatever Gregor had taught her, Tania knew that there were few pertinent facts available and everything should be considered. Marcus had heard the recording of Mary Valley's voice while she was under the narcotic and surely there would be written notes as well. Haynes must have put down a full description of the case and it would almost certainly have included an account of his first meeting with Anna Harb. During that interview, might not the woman have let slip that she was a member of some society which liked to keep its secrets well hidden. If that was the case, Haynes's notes might prove that the solution of her vanishing act would not be found on Bala, but less than five miles away.

'Sorry, Gregor, my dear.' Tania smiled as she opened the wardrobe and took out a coat. 'Like your acquaintance, Charles Kirk, I am only following a hunch and you would be very angry with me. All the same you are not my boss any more so get on and cultivate your garden.' She walked over to the telephone and the directory which would give her the address of Peter Haynes.

The flat was in a middle-aged block built shortly before the war and, judging by the few lights in its windows, was mainly tenanted by business people who needed a bed in London but returned to the country at the week-ends. There was an anonymous, indifferent atmosphere about the place, a feeling of 'come and go and we couldn't care less', and this was to Tania's advantage because the hall porter didn't even look up from his newspaper as she walked past his desk to the stairs. To him, tenants were probably mere numbers and names to be disregarded as long as the rent was paid on time and no complaints made.

Number 16. Peter Haynes's flat and her luck still held. She had feared that the door might have a mortice lock, but there was only a cheap spring device and plenty of space between the frame and the warped door. The strip of stiff plastic she had brought with her slipped easily through the gap, found the tongue of the lock and, with hardly any pressure the light spring was pushed back. Tania stepped into the unlighted hall, closing the door quietly behind her, and then paused as she smelt a tang of stale pipe smoke, heard a chair creak and saw that she was not alone. The lights were on in the sitting-room opposite and a huge, hunched figure was bent over a table with the ribbons of an eye shade around its massive forehead.

'You're back with them already, Alfie?' The man glanced at his watch. 'Good lad. Less than an hour from door to door. Keep up this display of speed and strict attention to duty and in time you may become even as I am.' He chuckled and raised a glass. Half a bottle of rum lay at his side and the table was littered with papers.

'I am afraid I am not Alfie, Mr Forest.' Tania had hoped to shock this unwelcome intruder, but she was disappointed. John Forest merely looked up mildly, turned the desk light towards her and smiled.

'No, I can see that, my dear Lady Levin. Alfie is a male child of sixteen and is undersized for his age. He also suffers badly from acne, poor lad.' Forest eyed Tania's ample figure with open appreciation and then saw the strip of plastic she still held and chuckled again, his jowl joggling up and down like a turkey's.

'Tch, tch, dear lady. A spot of housebreaking, eh, and by the most common method that television advertises. I've never really believed that it worked in practice. Your good gentleman, Sir Marcus, would be shocked to learn of such conduct.'

'How did you get in, Mr Forest?' Tania did not share Kirk's dislike of Forest. She was not particularly fond of him, but sometimes found him amusing. 'And what are you doing here anyway? I thought you had been injured and were still in hospital in Scotland.'

'I was injured, my dear. Gravely injured.' A flabby hand pointed to a strip of sticking plaster beneath the eye shade. 'I was stunned, concussed, hurled bleeding to the deck of the ferry boat like the proverbial stuck pig and like to die. But duty is a strict mistress and she has called me away from my bed of pain at Torar. While Sir Marcus, General Kirk and all the rest of the Uncle Tom Cobbleighs are busily pursuing ghosts on Bala, I felt that my talents would be better employed down here.

'But how rude of me. Let me offer you some liquid refreshment.' Forest pulled himself heavily out of the chair and lumbered across the room. 'The late Dr Haynes—sorry, Mr Haynes; the poor fellow was only a bachelor of medicine—has left us comfortably provided for. Would a gin and tonic be to your liking? Excellent.' He opened a cupboard and poured out a generous measure.

'As to your first question, I got in by the simple expedient of a five-pound note which will naturally be put down to expenses. Hall porters are not wealthy men and the old boy downstairs was only too delighted to lend me his pass key. Cheers.' Forest had handed her the glass and raised his own.

'And now, dear lady, may I ask what brings you here?'

'A hunch, Mr Forest, nothing more.' Tania sat down facing him. 'I'll try to explain, but please don't laugh at me because I only have a vague suspicion.' Tania told him about the theory she had considered in her bedroom and at every sentence she waited for him to shake his head or smile because it sounded quite absurd when repeated to another person.

'I see. You considered that Harb belonged to some league practising black magic and may have found friends and protectors on Bala.' Forest did shake his head when she had finished, but he didn't smile. His face was serious and thoughtful and he stared down at the rum as if some secret might be hidden in the amber liquid.

'Not at all a bad notion; quite as feasible as anything old Kirk managed to dream up and parts of it can possibly be substantiated.

'But before I put my cards on the table, may we make it Tania and John? If we are to collaborate it would be much more pleasant.

'Thank you, Tania.' He beamed at her nod and then squinted down at the papers before him.

'Great minds think alike, as they say, and it is clear to me that the Harb woman is either dead or will be captured in the very near future. Bala is crawling with reporters and neither her arrest nor the discovery of her body would make a major scoop. The early part of the story might however, and that is why I returned to London. Like you I was curious about the occult side of Madame Harb's career and what had caused the child's mental disturbance. Why was Peter Haynes the only person to notice it while the orphanage doctor stated the girl was perfectly normal? Could the answer lie in something that happened before the coach accident? From Haynes's notes we know that Anna Harb went to the hotel to see her daughter and the child failed to recognize her. Could that be only partly true? Did Mary in fact recognize her mother but was so frightened of her that her conscious mind rejected the knowledge?' Forest picked up his pipe, not lighting it, but turning the bowl round in his fingers as if the feel of the wood helped him to concentrate.

'What had been done to Mary, John?' Once again Tania felt a sudden spasm of nausea. 'What methods did that woman use on her to . . . ?'

'To plant occult powers in her brain.' Tania had broken off for loss of a word and Forest smiled; a small, grey smile that looked quite out of place in his fat, jovial face. 'God knows, Tania. But the point is this: it seems clear to me that she may have succeeded.

'No, Haynes did not even consider the possibility. I have been through his notes very carefully and there is nothing in them to support our theories, I'm afraid.' The chair creaked under his weight as Forest leaned forward over a sheet of typescript.

'Haynes was just a practical, unimaginative man of science, though a very worried one. He was so concerned about Mary's condition, which he describes as a memory lesion which would lead to physical schizophrenia in early puberty, that he was ready to go to any lengths to achieve a cure. He knew the risks he was taking in bringing Anna Harb to Saint Bede's, but they were calculated risks because he felt that the shock of their meeting might bring the child's illness to the surface. As we know all too well, he was completely wrong. It was the mother, not the child, who received the shock and that is why an army of men are hunting her down at this moment.

'Excuse me, though. That must be my young assistant.' There was a knock on the outer door and Forest walked off to answer it. Tania heard a laugh, a short mutter of conversation and when he returned he had a thick folder under his arm.

'Now, let's look at the early facts for a little, Tania.' He laid the file on the table and rummaged through it as he talked. 'A mentally deranged woman with claims of possessing occult powers who attempted to pass those powers on to her daughter. That child is later removed from her care and handed over to the Van Traylen Fellowship where she becomes the special favourite of Mrs Van Traylen and was staying at her house when Helen Van Traylen killed herself. Then, almost exactly a year later, we have the accident to the coach, Mary's admission to the hospital and Haynes's fears that she was mentally disturbed. Finally Anna Harb's visit to Mary, the death of Haynes and her attempt to kill or abduct Mary whom she described as "The soul that should not have been born."' Forest had found the section he was looking for at last and he pushed the rest of the papers to one side.

'Peter Haynes may have been a cold-blooded scientist, Tania, but he made one rather odd statement about Mary. He said that she appeared to be remembering something she could not possibly have experienced. It was that which really aroused my interest in his notes before you arrived like a thief in the night.' He gave another sad smile and walked over to a tape-recorder across the room. 'It also gave me a possible clue to what happened in the room to drive Anna Harb berserk. Did she realize that she had trained her daughter too well and produced a monster perhaps?' Forest had been rewinding a roll of tape and he motioned Tania across to him.

'That was the office file on the Van Traylen Fellowship which arrived just now, my dear. It contains a short biography of each of the society's guardians, but there is only one of these which need concern us, I fancy. While I am looking through it, I'd like you to listen to this tape which Haynes made of Mary Valley's reactions under narco-analysis.' He switched on the set and returned to the table.

'You are beginning to wake up, aren't you, Mary?' Peter Haynes sounded gentle, but also commanding. 'I want you to listen to me very carefully indeed, Mary. Last time after I put you to sleep you woke up and told me about somebody named Vincent. What happened to Vincent, Mary?'

'He died, sir. Vincent died long ago at Harmer Flats and I don't want to talk about him.' The child's voice had a whine and a sob in it. 'Please don't make me think about Vincent.'

'You must think about Vincent, Mary. I want to help you and you are going to tell me everything. You say that he died at a place called Harmer Flats. How did he die?'

'He burned . . . screaming . . . with the steers pushing him back . . . trampling his body . . . but still alive in the fire.' The words were punctuated by short gasps and so low that Tania could hardly hear them.

'And where were you, Mary? Did you see Vincent die?'

'Of course. I was there with him. I loved Vincent but I killed him too because it was my idea. We had to destroy the accounts before the auditors were due. A million dollars they would have found we owed in Federal tax and it seemed so simple . . . so very simple till the wind veered round to the north. No, let me sleep again. I don't want to talk about hell fire any more.'

'You must talk, Mary. You must let me help you.' Haynes spoke very slowly and Tania could almost feel him willing the child to talk. 'How did you start the fire?'

'We used kerosene, of course. The office building was mainly wood and it burned like a torch. And then the wind changed and the steers stampeded.' There was a long pause and when the voice returned it sounded resigned and Tania knew that Haynes must have broken through Mary's resistance.

'The wind swung round to the north, didn't it, my darling? It sent the flames right across the knocking pens and the plant itself caught fire. Then the steers broke out of the stockade and came towards us. I can still see them, hear them, even smell them in the smoke. Do you remember how red the horns looked, Vincent?' There was a child's scream, a woman's cry and then a grunting, bellowing sound that was not human at all.

'So you died, my darling, darling Vincent. You held them back till I had time to reach the truck and you died for me, my own darling. They gored you and trampled you and they threw you alive into the fire.' An old voice came whispering out from the tape-recorder and Tania felt a sudden stab of pain and looked down to see that her nails had dug deeply into the palms of her hands.

'You gave me my life, Vincent, and I swore I would always keep it safe for you. It was so cool in the truck at first. We used it to carry the pay rolls and the door was armoured; two-inch steel. Very slowly the heat came and then faster and faster till my body started to melt and I saw the door glow red. Yes, as red as a cherry the steel was and my body melted. Where are you, darling? Why don't the men come to help me?' An old woman broke off in a fit of sobbing and then the child's voice returned.

'Let me go home now please, sir. I want to go back to my friends and be safe with Auntie Alison and Uncle Michael and the others. Please don't send me back into the fire . . . into hell again.'

'Very soon you will go home, Mary.' There was a scraping sound as if Haynes had drawn his chair closer to the cot. 'But you must finish the story first. Who were the men who should have come to help you?'

'My men, our men, of course. Frank and Sean and Jesse; all of them. You saved my life at the end, Jesse, but you were still too late. I covered my face when I fell, but look at what happened to me. Look at my feet and my breasts and my poor, poor arms.'

'All right, Mary.' Haynes's voice was merely tired and the air of command had left it. 'That's all you can take for the present, so sleep well, my dear.' There was a click and then complete silence, except for the whirr of the tape running on to the end of the spool.

'Well, I've heard it, John.' Tania switched off the tape-recorder and walked over to the table. She felt drained of strength as if her body were a torn rag doll from which the sawdust stuffing was running out.

'That was not merely a nightmare or a story she had read or heard told to her. That child was actually experiencing something that had happened to her.'

'No, not to her personally, Tania.' Forest was staring dully at a sheet of newsprint and a photograph laid in front of him. 'Until a few moments ago I was a sceptic, Tania. I believed in the possibilities of clairvoyance and in extrasensory perception, but only in the possibilities. Not for one moment would I have admitted of such a thing as supernatural possession; that the spirits of the dead may enter into the living. Now, I am not sure. I am not sure about anything any more. I fear the supernatural and I don't like this, Tania.' He pushed the cutting and the photograph across to her and leaned far back in his chair, staring up at the ceiling.

'I've seen her before.' Tania studied the picture. Helen Van Traylen had been middle-aged when it was taken and she was still strikingly beautiful. She wore the same elbow-length gloves that Marcus had noticed in the other photograph.

'U.S. HORROR.' The newspaper clipping was so faded that Tania had to hold it under the lamp, 'MILLIONAIRE BURNED TO DEATH AS CATTLE STAMPEDE. NARROW ESCAPE OF SOCIETY HOSTESS.'

'Very strange, isn't it, Tania?' Forest was refilling his glass as he spoke. 'Haynes states that on the surface Mary Valley appears quite normal. It is only when she imagines she is unobserved, asleep or under drugs, that the condition is apparent. Only then does the obsession with heat and a dream of flames and pain and stampeded cattle and a man called Vincent take place.' His hand reached out and tilted Tania's face towards his own.

'Vincent has a surname, too. It was Van Traylen and he died during a fire which occurred in a meat-canning factory at a town called Harmer Flats in the American Middle West. His widow's name was Helen and she always wore long gloves to conceal the scars of her escape.

'I don't like it, my dear. I've always gone by facts and definite evidence and I've never written a story about the occult in my life. This is absurd, hocus-pocus, mumbo-jumbo and the three-headed devil howling on top of a ruined church.'

'But we have facts, John, three of them.' Tania drew back before the reek of rum on his breath. 'We know that Mary's mother claims to have occult powers and tried to pass them on to her daughter. We know that Mary was Mrs Van Traylen's special favourite and was in the house when the woman killed herself. I have just listened to the third fact and this confirms it.' She looked down at the date on the newspaper clipping.

'Possession is the only explanation there can be. How else could a small child relive something that happened to a dead woman more than thirty years ago?'

Chapter Fifteen

'TANIA DARLING, please listen to me. You must put this notion out of your mind.' Tania had telephoned him back a few minutes ago and Marcus was sitting behind the porter's desk of the Ben Deargh Hotel and shouting to make himself heard. The Home Secretary's ban on tourist traffic to Bala had come too late and every hostelry on the island was crammed to overflowing. There were the eager and public-spirited who had come to help, the merely curious and the openly morbid who hoped to witness a bloodthirsty climax. All these people had flocked over from the mainland and conditions at Lochern were chaotic. The Ben Deargh itself resembled a refugee camp, with camp beds in the corridors, and the entrance hall was like a railway booking office during the rush hour.

'You must remember that you are seven months pregnant, Tania, and have far too much imagination at any time. You've also been reading little except books on psychic research for the last year and they have obviously gone to your head. Please try and relax, my sweet. I realize you're distressed and have had to wait several hours to get in touch with me. But the military have taken over the exchange and it's a wonder you got a line at all. Tania, can you hear me?

'Damnation.' The telephone was silent and Marcus pressed the rest up and down impatiently. He was very anxious indeed about his wife and he cursed himself for leaving her in the first place.

'Operator, I was talking to a London number. 176 7832 and we've been cut off. Would you reconnect me, please?

'Yes, I do realize that all your lines are busy, but I am a doctor of medicine and this is urgent. Please, operator.

'Thank you. I'll hold on then.' Marcus edged himself still farther into the corner as two well-dressed, middle-aged women who should have known better started to hammer on the counter in the vain hope of finding accommodation.

Why did that blasted fellow Forest have to distress Tania with such an idea? he thought. She was a strong, healthy woman, but she might be in for a bad attack of pre-natal tension if this went on. He'd take the first available plane back to London and put an end to such notions at once.

And what a notion it was! The mind of a dead woman possessing a child and making her relive a terrifying experience which had happened years ago. Absurd, utterly untenable, and also revolting. As his many enemies said, Forest had been writing sensational muck for so long that he'd believe anything. He not only wrote clichés; he lived them.

'No, madam, I am not one of the hotel servants.' Marcus scowled up with a jerk as one of the women prodded him painfully on the shoulder with her umbrella. 'I am sorry your former accommodation was so uncomfortable that you had to give it up, but can assure you that there is not a bed to be found here. My advice is that you catch the last ferry back to the mainland. It leaves at seven o'clock.

'Thank you, operator. Yes, I'm still holding.' Through the open doors Marcus heard a rattle like machine-gun fire and watched a helicopter come wheeling over the opposite buildings and land in the square. The sun had set long ago and aircraft would be useless in the dark. In Marcus's own mind the whole search was of purely academic interest now. He and Kirk had spoken to the colonel of the marine commandos and he had been quite certain of that. With the exception of one small area, due to be beaten in the morning, the whole of Bala had been covered. There was little chance of Harb having managed to double back to the mainland and no chance at all of her being hidden by the local population, whatever Tania and Forest might dream up. The driver of the police car must have been correct in saying that her body was deep in the earth or out to sea.

But why had the authorities allowed civilians to pour on to Bala and create this state of chaos and hysteria? Marcus winced as one of the women found a bell and started to ring it loudly, while from outside the noise of the helicopter was replaced by a roar of motor cycles and a dozen youths in leather jackets shot across the square. The Van Traylen people were not the only ones who were suffering now. At this moment, a perfectly inoffensive gipsy woman was lying critically ill in the Cottage Hospital, having been beaten and kicked and slashed by a party of thugs who had mistaken, or claimed to have mistaken her for Anna Harb. There were some less seriously injured in the hospital too: the victims of a pitched battle between soldiers and two teenage gangs from Glasgow who had united against them.

'Madam, will you please stop ringing that blasted bell? I have no idea where the receptionist is, but I am sure she is being run off her feet. I have also told you that there are no vacant rooms in this hotel and you will have to sleep in the open, if you miss that ferry. For your further information I have heard the weather forecast which stated the night will be wet and cold.

'Operator? Of course I'm here. You can only allow us two minutes? Very well, but please put me through at once.

'Is that you, darling?' There was a series of clicks and squeals and then he heard his wife's voice. 'Tania, they are going to cut us off for good in a couple of minutes so please listen carefully. I don't want you to be alone tonight, so get Mrs McDoggart to sleep in. Better still ring Georgie Brown or the Stonehams and ask if they can put you up. I'm going to catch the next boat to the main-land and get on the first plane to London. I should be back with you some time in the morning.

'No, darling, please put that possession theory right out of your mind. I saw Mary Valley myself yesterday afternoon and I talked to the orphanage doctor. The child was badly shocked by the coach accident and that's all there is to that. Poor Peter Haynes made an absurd diagnosis and the little girl is quite normal.

'Tania, we'll talk about that tape-recording as soon as I see you, but do forget about it for the time being. I promise you that there is a perfectly rational explanation.

'Please, please, madam.' He glowered at the bell ringer who had resumed her efforts. 'Darling, it is quite obvious what hap-pened. Dr Rose told me that Mrs Van Traylen almost regarded Mary as her own daughter and she was a sick woman with a pain-ful and inoperable growth. Surely it is feasible that, in her distress, she told the child about her experience and, when Mary learned of the suicide, it became lodged in her subconscious.

'Tania, are you listening?' Marcus joggled the rest again, but the line was quite dead and he replaced the receiver.

'Yes, you heard me correctly, ladies.' The woman had lowered the bell and they both smiled at him. 'I am leaving tonight, but I have a double room with a friend who is staying on. No, I'm afraid he is not a gentleman and I doubt if he would vacate out of chiv-alry. I am also quite sure that he would not relish sharing his bed with either of you.' He gave them a courtly bow and shouldered his way into the bar where he had arranged to meet Kirk.

Though Anna Harb was a monster, she had certainly done a lot of good for the tradespeople of Lochern. The bar was crowded from end to end and most of the clients appeared to be drink-ing heavily: young army, naval and air force officers, groups of newspaper reporters and a cluster of campers in brightly coloured anoraks and heavy boots. Most of them were talking loudly and all were concerned with the subject of the chase.

'Yes, we've covered Sections K, L, M and N up to now and cordoned them off. That leaves only O and it's flat open country with no cover to speak of. The C.O. says he's convinced the woman has either managed to leave the island or is dead. All the same, I'm not so sure myself and between the three of us I'm looking forward to the morning. 06.00 hours we assemble and I shouldn't be a bit surprised if we don't flush her out. Tally ho, eh. Thanks, I would like a refill. A pink gin and ask him to put in a spot more angostura this time.'

'Cheers, gentlemen. Yes, it was a good story while it lasted. Got some cigarettes on you, Mr Murray, I seem to have come without my case?'

Marcus was wedged between the military and the roar of the Press: three prosperous-looking gentlemen on national dailies, the representative of the *Nordwest deutsche Tagesblatt*, and a crushed youth from the *Inner Isles Clarion and Advertiser*.

'Did you see my article yesterday? The chief was delighted. Sent me a personal telegram of congratulation. Let's have a light, Mr Murray.'

'Pity old Fattie Forest got in first, though. I was hoping that the capture and a few pictures might make him feel pretty silly about dashing back to the "Smoke", but there's little chance of that, apparently. I was talking to one of the helicopter pilots this afternoon and he's convinced the woman must be dead and all they'll find is a body. Still, while there's life, there's death, eh, and we'll just have to content ourselves with a corpse. Thanks, I'm alight, Mr Murray, but shove over those olives, there's a good chap.'

'What about another round, gentlemen? No, no, keep your hand out of your pocket, Bill. Surely it must be Mr Murray's turn? Of course it is. Mr Murray will get them. That'll be the three whiskies, a brandy and whatever you're drinking yourself, Mr Murray.

'I beg your pardon. Yes, naturally doubles and I rather think Herr Krebs would like a cigar. Let's have some sandwiches too, while you're about it. Smoked salmon all right with you, gentlemen?

'Good. Five rounds of the salmon, Mr Murray, and we might as well have a few anchovies as a relish.'

'I'm terribly sorry, Sir Marcus. Are we holding you back from the water hole? Show a little respect, Mr Murray. Don't let a Nobel prize-winner go thirsty. Won't you join us, Sir Marcus? Mr Murray's in the chair.'

'It's very kind of you, but I'm waiting for a friend so I'll get my own.' Marcus bought a small whisky and carried it over to the single vacant seat beside the window which was flanked on either side by groups of aggrieved hill walkers.

'Free country; don't make me laugh. National Trust property, all the Blyven Range is, and they wouldn't let us go near it.'

'Come 'ere to 'elp the police and do our civic duty and they chase us off like bleeding dogs.'

'Sod all rozzers and let's have another round, lads.'

They are enjoying themselves, Marcus thought, as he stared around the room. Even the abject Mr Murray who was having to change a cheque at the bar had an eager, excited look in his eyes. Everybody had thrilled to the chase and everybody was disappointed that their quarry might be dead. Who was it who had praised fox hunting as a sport that provided half the excitement of a battle with only a tenth the danger? The fellow was obviously right, but a human being appeared to be a much more attractive adversary than a fox.

Poor Tania, though. He should never have left her in her advanced state of pregnancy; she had sounded almost hysterical on the telephone. Marcus glanced at his watch. Charles was late but, whatever happened, he intended to catch that ferry. He would finish this whisky, pack his bag and leave a note for him. The old boy would understand. He'd once told him that his own wife had had bad pre-natal neurosis while she was carrying his son and a lot of good it had done her. Marcus turned and looked out of the window at the dark hills and the sweep of the Atlantic all around them. Alan Kirk was a few charred bones locked in a rusty hull and Charles had no family at all.

Damn John Forest. Damn you too, my darling. Oh, Tania, I love you very much, but why must you let your imagination run wild all the time? The soul of a dead woman entering the mind of a child to pass on her memories and personality: a ridiculous and repulsive notion.

Cajal and Forbes and Lashley. Marcus frowned as the names suddenly occurred to him without any apparent reason. Why should he suddenly think of three scientists whose work had been quite unconnected with his own?

Yes, complete nonsense. Helen Van Traylen had told that child her story and it had become lodged in the back of Mary's mind till the shock of the accident and Haynes's drugs released the memory. Cajal and Forbes and Lashley.

The personality of a woman who had died old and in great misery entering the mind of a child. Preposterous! There was not a shred of proven evidence for psychic possession or communication by a sixth sense. The subject was only fit for consideration by cranks and wishful thinkers and the writers of fairy stories.

Ramon Cajal and Forbes and Lashley. They had not been cranks, but level-headed men of science. Tyrell too. A fourth name joined the others in his mind and Marcus suddenly recalled just such a fairy story which had frightened him as a child. The details were vague, but it concerned a young baby, an old man and a mountain. Eagles too. Somehow the eagles had been the instruments of salvation.

No, it was too far back. He couldn't remember the story, though he distinctly recalled the nightmares it had given him and how he had tossed and turned on the straw bed at the back of his father's little shop at Lemberg.

Time was getting on, however, and he would have to leave soon without waiting for Kirk if he hoped to catch the ferry. Marcus glanced at his watch and took another sip of whisky. The room was filled with smoke and smelled pleasantly of damp tweed and two big collies which were crouching under the next table, obviously disturbed by the influx of strangers. Their owner was an old man in a kilt whose bow legs looked far too frail to support him.

Rubbish! Marcus fought against a sudden theory but, as he did so, the rest of the fairy tale came back to him. The room behind his father's shop had been dark and bare, the rain rattled on the shutters, but the brightly coloured illustration of the book was clear in his mind's eye and he knew that, outside, the Polish steppes had reared up into mountains as high as the Alps. On one of those mountains a stunted figure was climbing. A gnome, old and bent and hideously deformed, was toiling up to the summit with a white bundle in his arms. He halted on the summit, unwrapped the bundle, took a deep breath and leaned forward to transfer his own evil spirit into the body of the child. Their mouths were almost touching when, out of the heavens, came the eagles.

'Cajal and Forbes, Lashley and Tyrell.' The last name was the one that mattered and Marcus spoke aloud to the consternation of the aged shepherd beside him. Something cracked, something burned, but he hardly noticed the broken glass or the blood and whisky dribbling down from his hand. He was on his feet, pushing his way out of the room and he had completely forgotten about the ferry. For the first time he knew that there might be a rational explanation for Anna Harb's sudden outburst of mania, for Mary Valley's terrors, for the death of Sidney Molson, for everything.

'My apologies, Tania, and to you too, Mr Forest,' he said to himself as he hurried out of the hotel and across the square towards the tiny hospital. 'You are the only people who managed to hit on what may be the truth and it took a fairy story to make me believe you.' He halted at the entrance and turned to blow a kiss in what he imagined was the direction of London. 'Oh, my good, clever Tania Valina Levin, I am so much in love with you.

'And thank you also, my dear colleagues. I know little of your work, but I may be indebted to you before long.' He followed the kiss with an ironic bow. 'Doctors Cajal and Forbes, and Tyrell and Lashley.'

Chapter Sixteen

'SHE IS dead, General Kirk. In my own mind there is not the slightest doubt about that, and I'm equally sure that we'll never find the body.' The walls of the laird's chalet-type residence were lined with sporting trophies and between an otter's pad and the mask of a dispirited-looking fox hung a glass-covered map of the island.

'And without a body, the story will turn into legend. For generations this island will remain a symbol of murder and insanity and witchcraft. Our tourist trade may well be wiped out and all we'll get will be morbid day-trippers to stare at us as if we were ghouls ourselves.

'Yes, Anna Harb has shot her bolt but the poison will remain.' Cameron's knuckles rapped the glass cover. 'You heard what Colonel Fenwick had to report, I believe. Only one section is left to be searched in the morning and that's Drummond Moor, over here. It's been under observation from the air and from the Blyven Ridge since yesterday and it provides no cover at all. A rabbit couldn't go undetected on the moor, let alone a human being. The woman is dead, and her story will remain to trouble Bala.

'May I refresh your drink, General?'

'No, no thank you, Chief Constable.' Kirk knew the power of the clear, innocent-looking Skye whisky and he slid a hand over his glass as Cameron approached with a bottle.

'But how can you be so certain that Harb is dead? It is still a comparatively short time since that little boy was murdered. Unless a body is found I think we must assume that she may be alive and the danger remains.'

'Because we will never find a body, General.' Cameron poured himself another generous measure. 'If you knew Bala as well as I do, you'd understand why I'm so sure about that. There are bogs and pitfalls and caves all over the island and a tide called the Scourie that sweeps between us and Raasay like a fast-flowing river. She's dead, and either deep in the earth or somewhere out in the Atlantic.

'Try and think about it dispassionately. Food and above all water she'd need and it's been a dry year. The burns are very low and every one of them and every lake is guarded. We found some of her clothing in the car, as you know, and the dogs have the scent. The bloody woman probably stank like a polecat and they haven't had a sniff of her.

'Just look at that now.' There was a sudden glow of light beyond the town and Cameron strode angrily out on to the veranda.

'Another blasted bonfire and our people will have had nothing to do with it. They are either good Catholics who share my view that Guy Fawkes should have had better luck, or pious Calvinists who disapprove of all idle celebrations. The whole place is crawling with hooligans from the mainland and most of my regular police have been taken off the hunt to control them. That'll be more of their work. We've had fighting in the bars, that poor gipsy pedlar assaulted and the attack on the soldiers. Now, they are obviously burning ricks and it's got to stop, General. Once Drummond Moor has been covered tomorrow and they've drawn a blank, I intend to issue a statement that Harb is dead and the emergency is over. They'll scurry back to the Glasgow rat holes where they belong once they think the fun is over.

'Quite sure you won't have another jar, General? This stuff never did anybody any harm, whatever that fool James Knight, our new G.P., has to say.'

'No thank you, I must be off in a moment, Chief Constable.' Kirk looked up at a clock on the mantelpiece. 'I'm meeting Marcus Levin at six thirty and time is getting on.'

'Well, it's your funeral.' Cameron downed his own drink and refilled the glass. 'Angus Sinclair, our good old doctor, said that pure malt spirit was the finest tonic there is when taken in moderation. But he retired last year and this young English pup, Knight, took over the practice. I went to see him not so long ago because I've been having a bit of trouble with me guts. The fellow had the impudence to suggest it might be due to my drinking habits. He even joked about it and said I was suffering from a condition known as "Publican's bile".' Cameron glanced at the bottle with a frank plea in his eyes.

'You might ask your pal Levin what he thinks about that, General. Surely there's no harm in it; not good pure whisky taken in moderation and if you eat well.'

'I'll certainly mention it to him, Chief Constable.' Kirk was leaning against the balustrade and staring at the glow across the bay.

'Fire,' he said to himself. 'Mary Valley is both attracted and repelled by fire.'

'That's it, General. Right first go, which proves what a fool young Knight is.' His host nodded in agreement. 'You obviously suffer from the same complaint, though you seem to be a most modest drinker. Every morning it's as if there was a ruddy great fire in my guts, burning the innards; horrible. Then, whenever I go to the heads, it's like passing razor blades.'

'I'm sorry. I'm sure your symptoms are most objectionable, Captain Cameron, but I was thinking of something else.' Kirk walked back into the room and studied the wall map. 'The daughter is fascinated by fire and I'm wondering if the mother has the same fascination. This evening, the orphanage children are being given a party with a bonfire and fireworks. Do you think it possible that that might bring her out?'

'No, I do not, for the simple reason that I am convinced the woman is dead; buried in a bog or swept out to sea.' Cameron shook his head in irritation. 'But even if she is alive, she couldn't possibly get anywhere near Inver House. There are pickets right across the peninsula, as you have seen for yourself, General; here, here and here.' He pointed at the map. 'Nobody could possibly get past them, even at night, and I've also got dog handlers patrolling the walls.'

'I am not worried about her getting in.' Kirk tried to recall the layout of the orphanage. A wall which was approximately eight feet high, grounds with trees and shrubs, the playing field ending at the edge of the cliff, which he had considered horribly danger-ous for children, and a flight of steps running down to the jetty from which the launch had put out on its last voyage. The main block itself with imitation turrets and battlements towering over the paved quadrangle and at least a dozen minor buildings dotted around it; garages and store-houses and sheds.

'If you are wrong and Anna Harb is alive, it seems probable that the only place where she could be hiding is Inver House itself.'

'Good God, General.' Cameron brought his fist crashing down on a table. 'Though they wouldn't let us station men inside the grounds, the Van Traylen people have searched every nook and cranny of the place themselves. They are completely confident the woman is nowhere on their premises. If they're not worried, why should you be?'

'Because of a little girl's fascination with fire, Chief Constable.' An unpleasant picture had formed in Kirk's mind. The cheerful glow of the bonfire, the sound of fireworks, children laughing and shouting and old people who were trying to forget their fears and sorrows. Then, out from some dark cranny might come a woman. A monster creeping stealthily out to kill again.

'Just another hunch, but all the same, I would rather like to go to the orphanage this evening, so if you will excuse me . . .'

'Please yourself, General Kirk. Go to Inver House and play watchdog if you're so minded. But it's blowing up for a foul night so don't expect me to accompany you. I've done everything I can to protect those people and I'm quite sure they're not in any further danger.' He sat down and scribbled a note as Kirk put on his coat and muffler. 'Take this to the police station and they'll lay on transport. We don't want you wandering about on your own and ending up in hospital with that poor gipsy.' Cameron handed Kirk the paper and led him to the door feeling extremely disgruntled.

'Bloody old fool.' He returned to his sitting-room, muttering aloud as he poured out another tot of the harmless, pure malt spirit. 'The blasted woman is dead and this business has driven everybody round the bend. She must be dead because no other explanation is possible.' The telephone rang and he scowled as he answered it.

'Oh, it's you, Inspector. Well, what's the news? More outrages by those Glasgow hooligans, I suppose.'

'Yes, sir. They've set a rick alight near Fula Bay, but that's not why I'm ringing.' The policeman's voice was slightly guarded. 'I am speaking from the hospital and Sir Marcus Levin is with me. He has just told me a rather strange theory and wishes to examine the medical evidence. But Dr Knight is here as well and he refuses to co-operate.'

'Then make him co-operate, Inspector. Marcus Levin is a very eminent man.' Kirk's sudden departure still ruffled the Chief Constable and the very mention of the offending Knight increased his ill-humour. 'Good God, Grant, can nobody take any action without me holding his hand? Have I to be a wet nurse to the whole blasted island?'

'Of course not, sir, but if you would just listen for a moment, I think you will agree that you should come down here. What Sir Marcus suggests is that . . .' Grant spoke more firmly now, and in spite of his temper Cameron did listen. But not for very long. After hearing five sentences, he let the telephone fall from his hand, knocked back the whisky in a single gulp and hurried out of the house without bothering to put on his coat.

Chapter Seventeen

'I am sorry, Sir Marcus, but I cannot follow your reasoning at all.' Dr James Knight was a young man with a deep sense of grievance which had made him arrogant and suspicious. In time he might become a useful G.P., but he had only been at Lochern for six months and found the going extremely rough. The local people distrusted him because he was English, and since he had fallen foul of the laird his practice had been halved.

'We know the exact time and manner in which these unfortunate people died. They were killed by an explosion of petrol and dynamite which you yourself witnessed, Sir Marcus. Why should you wish to examine their remains now?'

'Because no proper autopsy has been performed on them, Doctor. That may not have been thought necessary at the time, but I would like to make a certain test on the bodies now.'

'Autopsy! Bodies!' Marcus had spoken quietly, almost with a plea in his voice, but Knight scowled at him. His hospital appointment had been made automatically when he bought the practice from its former occupant and he felt it was the one thing he could still call his own. Now a London specialist had joined the locals to flaunt his authority and was bearding him in his own den.

'Don't you realize that there was nothing that you could call a body, Sir Marcus? The police consider that approximately three pounds of dynamite were detonated on the launch. Isn't that right, Inspector? All that was brought here were shattered fragments and only one man could be identified because he happened to have a tattoo mark on his right forearm which was recovered.

'No I did not perform an autopsy, Sir Marcus, and there was not the slightest reason why I should have done so.'

'But the bodies . . . Sorry, Doctor. The fragments of human tissue which were recovered are still in your keeping and were placed in cold storage as soon as they were brought to you.' Marcus fully understood Knight's feelings and he forced himself to appear friendly. 'All I am asking is that you allow me to examine some of that tissue.'

'No, I would prefer not to give you detailed reasons at this point, Doctor. I have mentioned my theory to the Chief Constable and Inspector Grant and they are agreed that the tests should be made. But, at the moment, it is only a suspicion, and I would much rather not commit myself.'

'Listen to me, Knight.' Cameron and the Inspector had been silent witnesses up to the present, but now the laird decided to lend a hand.

'I am aware of your professional qualifications, but I also know that Sir Marcus Levin is an internationally respected scientist. He has made a perfectly reasonable request and I am ordering you to grant it.'

'Please let me finish.' Marcus tried to break in, but Cameron raised his voice to silence him.

'I happen to be Chief Constable of this island, its most important landowner and the Chairman of the County Council, Doctor, and I am going to make you a firm promise. Enough time has been wasted already, and unless you agree to co-operate with Sir Marcus immediately I shall see that your appointment to this hospital is not renewed and that you lose the few remaining patients you still have. Is that clear, Doctor?'

'Perfectly clear, Captain Cameron.' The young man flared back at him. 'From the day I told you the truth about your physical condition your attitude towards me has not only been clear but openly hostile. I have no doubt that you can bully your peasants into terminating my appointment, but for the time being I am in charge here. Now, will you please leave this building before I have you thrown out?'

'Oh, try and grow up, Dr Knight.' Marcus's voice was suddenly strident and foreign; Israel wailing at the petty squabbles of Aryans. 'We are professional colleagues, remember, and I am asking for your co-operation as one colleague to another. There was not the slightest reason why you should have performed an autopsy. Nobody is criticizing you in any way, so please get that into your head. All I want is to be allowed to make a few simple tests and, as a colleague, I think you should have the good grace to help me.'

'Very well, Sir Marcus. If you put it like that, I will do what you want, though I still think it is a complete waste of time. Please come this way, gentlemen.' The repetition of 'colleague' had done the trick and Knight was mollified at last. He led them across to a room which obviously served as both laboratory and operating theatre, nodded to a sister on duty and then turned to Cameron.

'You heard what Sir Marcus said, Captain Cameron? That I had no reason to perform an autopsy because the time and causes of death were obvious. That no blame can be attached to me.'

'Naturally I heard, Doctor.' The laird gave a curt nod. 'Nobody is criticizing your conduct in any way, and I apologize for my outburst just now. But for God's sake get on with it, man. If Sir Marcus's suspicions prove to be correct, we'll have to act on them quickly.'

'Of course.' The apology had completely restored Knight's good humour. 'What do you wish to examine, Sir Marcus? As I told you we were unable to piece together a single complete body.'

'What I want is a small section of cerebral tissue, Doctor.' Marcus glanced around the room. 'I don't suppose you happen to have a high-magnification microscope I could use?'

'We have indeed. Sister Angus will get it for you.' He turned and hurried out of the door and Marcus crossed over to the sister who was already lifting the instrument from a shelf below the bench. He had not expected to find such a thing on Bala and this was a recent German model and exactly what he needed.

'Thank you, Sister. That is a very nice piece of machinery indeed.' He smiled at the girl, noticing the strange mixture of races in her face: the dark hair of the Celt merging with a fair skin and pale-blue eyes handed down from some Viking pirate.

'Now, all I will need is a few slides, a scalpel and some stain; gentian violet would be best. And a devil of a lot of luck, Sister.' Though Marcus smiled, he did not feel cheerful at all. Like Kirk waiting for the computer reading, he hoped that his suspicions were completely groundless. If they were, he would merely have earned the scorn of Knight and Cameron and Grant and that was unimportant. But if he were correct, if Tania's hysterical theory on the telephone had put him on the right lines, then he would have proved that Anna Harb was not the only source of evil and the real enemy was Legion.

How he wished that Tania was with him. From outside a ship's siren bellowed three times; the ferry boat which would have started him on the journey back to London. If only Charles was here. Why did the old boy have to go rushing off to the orphanage without even leaving him a message? Presumably Kirk knew his own business best, but it would be nice to have his reassurance now: to have somebody to tell him that his suspicions were groundless; that there were no devils, no possession, no force of darkness walking the earth. Once again Marcus had a clear image of the illustration which had troubled his childhood. A bent, deformed figure toiling up a mountain and, high above it, the wings of the circling eagles.

'Here we are, Sir Marcus.' Knight had returned and laid a sealed container on the bench. 'Sister Angus given you all you need?'

'She has indeed.' Marcus unscrewed the metal top, smelling a faint tang of antiseptic as he peered down at what had once been part of a man: George L'Eclus, amateur yachtsman, racehorse owner, millionaire and philanthropist.

'Scalpel please, Sister.' He prepared a specimen carefully while the nurse switched on the lamp and Cameron and the policeman craned forward like children waiting for a conjuror to produce his first rabbit.

'I understand that L'Eclus was not only the sole victim to be identified, but the first to be recovered, Doctor.' Marcus laid the slide in position and turned the fine adjustment. Salt water, chemicals and refrigeration had done their work well, but the picture was rather beautiful—an action painting of shrivelled cells and blood corpuscles stained a light purple by the dye. They told him very little. 'How long was L'Eclus in the sea?'

'Under an hour, Sir Marcus. A fishing boat managed to pick him up almost immediately.' Knight was standing at his elbow with a look of complete bewilderment on his face. 'But I still don't understand. The man has been dead for two days. What do you expect to find?'

'I shall probably find nothing, Doctor. Forty-eight hours is a long time. All the same, for most of that period the tissue has been frozen and mortification would have been slowed down, if not arrested.

'No, this doesn't tell me a thing, I'm afraid. Just a moment, though.' Marcus had been about to remove the slide and prepare another when suddenly he stiffened, because there was something of interest. Nine-tenths of the picture were consistent with the evidence and showed nothing except the dead world of shrivelled tissue. But in the top right-hand corner there was a difference. The cells had a hard, almost metallic look about them which might tell him that his worst fears were justified. Only *might*, however. Marcus pushed emotion and loathing aside and concentrated on the job in hand. There was a hint of mummification present but no more.

'Good girl.' The sister had forestalled him by preparing another specimen and he exchanged the slides, feeling a trickle of sweat on his forehead and his heart beats speed up as he peered through the eyepiece. Because there was the proof clear before him. That was all he needed to know. The demons did exist and it had taken Tania's preoccupation with the occult to reveal their faces.

Cajal and Forbes and Tyrell and Lashley. The names of the four scientists raced through his head as he straightened from the bench and motioned Knight to take his place.

'Have a look for yourself, Doctor. The progress of the gangrene is rather significant, I think.' Marcus heard Knight give a low whistle of astonishment as he walked over to a wash basin and started to soap his hands very carefully.

'Well, Sir Marcus, what is it, man?' Cameron was flushed with impatience and irritation. 'Did you confirm your theory or not?'

'I am very sorry to say that I have confirmed it, Chief Constable.' Marcus was staring down into the basin. The hot water had dislodged the sticking plaster from the cut in his palm and was reddening with the blood.

'We know that this man, L'Eclus, was on the launch and his body was so mutilated that it could only be identified by a tattoo mark. That was almost exactly two days ago.

'Thank you, Sister.' He took a towel from her and dried his hands. 'The point is this, gentlemen. George L'Eclus was not killed at the time or in the manner you suppose. The condition of the brain tissue makes that quite clear. L'Eclus had been dead for at least twenty-four hours before the launch exploded.'

Chapter Eighteen

IT WAS an evening of contrasts. In the south and east the sky was clear and full of stars, but from the north, bars of dark cloud were moving inland like the spearheads of an advancing army.

'First time I've been up in these parts, sir, but I should say we're in for a blow before morning.' On his way to the police station for transport Kirk had thumbed a lift from an army truck and the officer at his side smiled happily. He had one pip on his battledress tunic and looked about sixteen years old. 'We're sleeping under canvas, as I told you, so a good storm will be something for the boys to remember.'

'You appear to have been enjoying yourself, Lieutenant.' The road to the peninsula was under repair and Kirk clutched the door as they rattled over the uneven surface.

'You're right about that, sir. We are part of a training unit, and for the last three months we've been stuck in barracks outside Carlisle. This has been a real break for us; almost like proper combat practice. Bit of a let down in the end of course.'

'How do you mean, Lieutenant?' Kirk turned away from the smiling face. Why did so many young men in uniform remind him of his son these days, he wondered bitterly, staring out at the wide sweep of the Atlantic. Alan had been dead for more than twenty-five years. He was at peace, buried safely under the ocean, and there was no point in torturing himself with the memory. All the same, how he wished that he was in a police car with a stolid, middle-aged driver and not beside this eager youth to bring back the past and trouble his memory. 'What is the let down, my boy?'

'That there's no chance of taking the woman alive, sir.' The young man saw the query in Kirk's face and shook his head. 'Oh, that's definite enough. Apart from the moorland section which they're beating at first light tomorrow morning, every surface yard of the island has been covered. The C.O. is certain that she must be dead or has left Bala, and we'll be on our way back to Carlisle in a day or two. Pity, but there you are and it was fun while it lasted, sir.'

'I suppose it must have been.' The general kept his eyes fixed on the lines of cloud hurrying in towards the hills. Good training for soldiers, he thought. News for reporters, exercise for the young men of the mountain rescue teams and an endless source of material for the writers of crime articles. The only price was ritual murder, mass murder and a group of old people who had been almost driven out of their minds by fear and sorrow.

Entertainment had been provided for louts too. The driver sounded his horn and in the headlights Kirk saw that the road ahead was blocked by a crowd of youths in leather jackets and crash helmets. Some of them were busily lighting fireworks which they clearly intended to use as grenades.

'Don't slacken speed, Corporal Jervis. Blow your horn, but keep your foot on the accelerator too and I'll take full responsibility for anything that happens.' The lieutenant's voice was full of excitement. 'Drive straight at 'em.'

'My pleasure, Mr Baxter. Your message clearly understood.' The driver's foot went down to the floor boards, the truck roared forward and Kirk braced himself for the crunch of metal on flesh. A shower of crackers exploded before the windscreen, Roman Candles flared and then, at the last possible moment, the jeering, capering ranks broke and scurried for safety like rats in a stubble field.

'Bastards! I wish you'd managed to get a couple of them, Jervis.'

The officer turned round to watch the abject figures pulling themselves out of the ditch.

'Did you hear what happened to that company of R.E.s last
night, sir? Twenty unarmed men attacked by over fifty louts with
knives and bicycle chains. I'll take the wheel on the way back, Corporal, and if there's any more trouble I intend to enjoy myself.'
He laughed in anticipation as the truck thundered on. The moon
was coming out from behind the mountains and the narrow lane
appeared like a ribbon stretched tightly across the dark moorland.

> Oh never fear, man, nought's to dread,
> Look not left nor right:
> In all the endless road you tread
> There's nothing but the night.

Kirk frowned as the quotation came to mind. He was the only
person who had wondered why Anna Harb should have quoted
Housman's 'soul that should not have been born' and now he
appeared to be the only person who considered that the woman
was still living and remained a threat. All of them, the police,
the military, Cameron and even Marcus were convinced that the
danger had passed. But somehow he knew that Anna Harb was
very much alive and tonight he would see her for himself.

'I'm afraid this is where we'll have to part company, sir.' A torch
was flagging them down and the lorry drew up beside a group of
soldiers. 'I'm to relieve these chaps and take them straight back to
Lochern.' Boots clattered as the relief party left the rear compartment and the lieutenant held out his hand.

'Goodbye, sir. Inver House is only about a third of a mile off
and you'll see it from the top of the next rise. I would have liked to
take you the whole way, but the adjutant is a bit of a tartar and my
orders are to get back as quickly as I can.'

'Don't give it a thought, my boy.' As their hands touched, the
khaki uniform seemed to turn blue and Kirk saw a young midshipman saying goodbye to him. 'With all those violent characters on
the prowl it was noble of you to pick me up in the first place. Good
night Mr Baxter, and thank you very much indeed.' Kirk climbed
down from the cab and started off along the road.

After what happened later, the general retained no single memory of his walk, but only a series of disjointed impressions. How bright the beaches looked in the moonlight; the approach of the belt of cloud driven by a breeze as steady and unfaltering as a trade wind; the lights of a trawler far out to sea and the constant call of gulls. Now and again he had the feeling that he was not alone and that a tall gaunt figure was creeping behind him, and twice he turned and looked back before shrugging his shoulders and striding on with Housman's reassurance in his mind. 'In all the endless road you tread there's nothing but the night.' He recalled the roughness of the tarmac through his thin city shoes, the constancy of the wind and his blind assurance that he was right and everybody else was wrong. Anna Harb was alive and he was walking towards her.

The lieutenant had underestimated the distance and Kirk had covered a good half-mile before he topped the ridge and saw the orphanage in front of him. The sun had been shining when he and Marcus had visited the place and even then they had found it sad. Now, in the gloom, Inver House had an air of utter defeat and helplessness, with its mock towers and battlements forlorn against the wild sky and the wall which would never keep out a determined enemy.

'Have you some form of identification on you, sir?' A police car was parked across the road and a uniformed serjeant climbed out.

'Thank you, General Kirk.' He shone a torch on the pass Cameron had written out and handed it back to him. 'That's quite in order, sir. If the laird says you're to go through, I won't stop you, though I don't know what sort of reception you'll get from them.' He nodded towards the gate. 'Time and again we've asked to put men inside and they've always refused. Dr Tyrell says they are quite capable of looking after themselves. Crazy, if you ask me, though there seems little doubt that the woman is dead.'

'Dr Tyrell?' The name rang a faint bell in Kirk's memory as he tucked away the pass.

'Oh, my mistake, General. That was her maiden name of course. She married an old chap named Rose a few years ago, but he died not so long back. Suicide it was; very sad. Dr Laura Rose you'll know her as, sir.

'Quite a party those kids seem to be having.' The serjeant was watching a rocket curve up over the headland and Kirk could smell woodsmoke. 'Personally I don't approve of such goings on. According to my beliefs it is mocking the Creator to burn one of his creatures in effigy.'

'Perhaps you're right, Serjeant.' Fire and explosives, Kirk thought, recalling the orange flare obscuring the launch and the wreckage crashing down on the deck of the ferry. Five sticks of dynamite were thought to have been stolen from the store and the experts believed that three would have been ample to produce the explosion. A guy; a dummy figure and a murderess who had proved her skill at sabotage.

'See you later, Serjeant.' Kirk considered asking the man to accompany him, but he had no evidence only suspicions and the police had orders to remain where they were. The main doors were locked, but there was a wicket gate to the right of them. He pushed his way in and set off along an overgrown path that led through a thicket of stunted trees and shrubs. More rockets soared over the mock towers of the big house in front of him and smoke was drifting inland on the steady breeze. Children and old people, they would all be together, grouped around the fire on the head-land and many things might be hidden in the body of a guy.

Would they listen to him, Kirk wondered as he hurried through the thicket: Michael Fawnlee, Eric Yeats, Rose / Tyrell, Grace Alison and the rest of the survivors? Could he make them understand that the orphanage was the only place in which their enemy could be hiding, and that Mary Valley's dreams of pain and violence came to her from a mother who was obsessed with fire? Could he persuade them that their bonfire would bring her out to wit-ness the final act of her bent crusade? Once again he recalled that orange flash and he pictured the loving care with which a group of children must have cut and stitched and filled a cloth figure with rags or sawdust. Then, while the children slept, had other hands, skilled in the use of explosives, opened the stitches and inserted a detonator and the remaining sticks of dynamite? Was the huntress already out in the open and could each stunted tree and bush he passed be hiding her? A crazed and completely merciless creature waiting to witness the deaths of her own child and the people who had stolen Mary from her.

Kirk was through the thicket now and he stepped out on to the quadrangle, his feet ringing on the cobbles and his breath coming in gasps. No more rockets were appearing over the buildings and he heard snatches of song drifting towards him. Soon would come the finale and they would be gathering closer to the fire, ready for the advent of the guy.

There was the bonfire in plain sight at last. Kirk pounded through an arch in the quadrangle and he could see its glow less than two hundred yards away from him across the playing field. They had built it close to the edge of the cliff and it might have been a beacon to warn sailors. A great stack of blazing, bone-dry timbers, with flames fanned by the steady breeze so that they licked over the grass towards the figures before them. The men and women stood a little way back, but the children were very close to the fire and appeared to dominate the proceedings. They had formed two separate groups; those nearest to him wearing normal clothes for their age, but the others had put on fancy dress which made them look like stunted adults. The boys were singing and the girls dancing in couples, and above them was the thing he had dreaded to see. Tied or strapped to a pole, a life-sized figure towered above the flames. The body was human, but the face was a pig's mask and the clothes stirred in the wind as if encasing a living creature. Two ropes held the pole back from the fire and Mary Valley was stationed beside one of them. In the firelight he could see that there was a knife in her hand and long black gloves covered her arms up to the elbows. Kirk had had to pause to regain his breath for a moment and, as he took in the scene, he realized that the child must have dressed up to resemble her dead benefactress, Helen Van Traylen.

Go on. You must go on, you idle old fool. Kirk's whole body was weak with exhaustion, but he forced himself forward, running faster than he had imagined possible. He was quite certain he knew what that grinning, pig-faced thing contained, and if even one rope was severed it would topple into the fire.

'No, no, no . . .' A hundred and fifty yards to go . . . a hundred and twenty . . . a hundred. He shouted as loudly as he could, but he knew that his voice was a croak and the wind was blowing the words away from them. His heart pounded in agony, his feet slipped and stumbled on the grass, but rage and horror forced him forward. A little girl who screamed at the very thought of fire, yet was also obsessed by it, a boy whose feet and hands had been pierced ritually and six old, broken bodies drifting out to sea. Now, straight in front of him was the last act, and he had to prevent that guy from falling.

'Mary, stop it. You must not cut the rope.' Seventy yards left and there appeared to be blood, not saliva in his mouth. But some of the children had seen him at last. They glanced indifferently at him for an instant and then turned and stared towards the fire again.

'Mary, listen to me.' Less than fifty yards, and he couldn't run any farther. He could do nothing except put every remaining ounce of strength into his voice and stagger slowly forward. 'Drop that knife, Mary. I order you to drop it.'

Mary Valley heard him, but all she did was to smile. She stood quite motionless, one gloved hand on her hip in a slightly coquett- ish stance, the other holding the knife firmly, and her little white teeth shone in the firelight as she watched him hobble towards her. She let him approach to within twenty yards and then the knife started to saw at the rope.

Kirk threw himself to the ground. His legs would no longer obey him, he had done all he could and it was finished. He gave one final croak of 'get back' as the ropes parted, the pole swayed and began to topple forward, and then he screened his face against the coming explosion. At almost the same moment he heard a sudden choking, gasping sob of agony and terror and he looked up again to see a sight that proved him completely and utterly wrong and which would haunt him for the rest of his days.

The wind had torn the cardboard mask from the face of the guy to reveal the human face that had been hidden behind it. He saw Anna Harb, with eyes and mouth wide open, fall screaming into the flames.

Chapter Nineteen

KIRK WAS old and weary and weak and it hadn't taken much to overpower him. Twenty pairs of small but capable hands had held him to the ground while children laughed and sang and a woman was burned alive. Now it was finished and Anna Harb was dead, buried deeply in the embers of the fire which still flared in the wind, constantly fed with fresh supplies of driftwood.

'You almost spoilt our party, General Kirk. Nobody is allowed to come here without an invitation.' They had bound his hands and feet and little Mary Valley frowned down at him. 'This is our home and I wanted my revenge to be private. It was very wrong of you to try and stop us.'

'You burned your own mother alive, Mary, and they allowed you to do it.' Kirk was kneeling on the ground with his back to the fire and the girl stood in front of him. At either side of Mary, the children were still stationed in their separate groups. Those in fancy dress looked bright and interested, enthralled spectators at some exciting entertainment, but the others appeared crushed and subdued and at least two of them were sobbing.

'They! The guardians! They would never stop me doing anything, General. After all I am the mistress here.' Mary half turned and nodded towards the buildings at the end of the field. The old people had drawn back there and stood with their heads bowed as if the proceedings had nothing to do with them.

'Listen to me, Mary. Listen to me carefully.' Kirk had to concentrate to form the words. He could still see that pole sway and then start to topple forward; slowly at first, as a tree falls, and then faster and faster till its living burden shrieked and scrabbled in the fire and then suddenly became still and there was nothing except the crackle of the flames, the steady drone of the wind and the shouts and laughter of children. The first part of his theory had been correct enough. After the murder of Sidney Molson, Anna Harb had hidden in the orphanage grounds, but she had been discovered and her intended victims had taken their own terrible revenge.

'You had every reason to hate and fear your mother, Mary, but you are ill, my dear. You don't know what you are doing and you need help. Anna Harb was a wicked woman. She killed Haynes and Sidney Molson and the people on the launch and many others. She may have intended to kill you too. But you should not have revenged yourself like that, Mary. That showed me that Mr Haynes was right in what he said. You need help very badly indeed, but they cannot give it to you.' He nodded towards the forlorn group of adults. 'What has happened, what has been done, has made them ill too and they cannot protect you any more. Now, I want you to untie me, my dear, and I will take you to people who can help.'

'You fool, General Kirk. Oh, you poor, stupid fool.' Mary Valley laughed. She threw back her head, chuckling and giggling, and then pirouetted round and round on the grass, the long dress swirling to show the chubby legs of a child. But somehow the glare of the flames made her face look old and bitter and diseased.

'You think Anna killed Haynes, General?' She stopped dancing and grinned at the embers at the bottom of the fire. 'You still don't understand anything, do you?

'I killed Haynes, General Kirk. He wanted to lock me up and separate me from my friends. Then he brought Anna to see me and they talked about mental disturbances at first and then about supernatural possession. They were still a long way from the truth, but getting closer so I had to stop them. I snatched Anna's great vulgar hatpin and stabbed Haynes between the eyes.

'Wasn't that clever of me? Anna was a convicted murderess and everybody was bound to blame her. After all, who would imagine that an innocent child of seven would do such a thing. Anna knew that and she lost her head. She dragged me out of the room and was going to hold me over the well of the stairs till I confessed what I had done. One day I really must thank Sir Marcus Levin for helping me, General.' She gave him a curtsy and another flashing smile. The white teeth were bright in the smooth, youthful face, but there was nothing youthful in the eyes above them. 'Do you understand now?'

'I am beginning to.' Haynes had diagnosed schizophrenia, Kirk remembered. Had that been only partly true and was there indeed such a thing as psychic possession? He glanced away from Mary to the children on her right. The boys all wore long trousers and the girls, flowing dresses and for a second time they made him think of stunted adults. 'But go on with the story, my dear. Anna was insane when she followed you here. She murdered the people on the launch and your friend Sidney Molson. But what about the others? The people before—Mrs Van Traylen, Colonel Anderson and the rest of them . . .'

'Oh, General Kirk, I thought you would have been an intelligent man, but you disappoint me so badly.' Mary shook her head and the long fair hair streamed out like flames before her. 'Anna arrived here three days before the launch was destroyed. She came at night with a hood to disguise her appearance and she talked to the guardians. She told them what I had done to Haynes and she asked them to help her prove her innocence.

'Can you imagine such stupidity, my friend? Anna did not realize that we are a Fellowship in every sense of the word.'

'They knew? They knew all the time and they did nothing?' Kirk stared in horror towards the bowed figures across the field. He had thought in terms of group mania but he suddenly realized what the truth might be and it was far worse than anything he had imagined.

'Of course they knew. And Anna was so useful to us. We kept her well hidden and she took the blame for the launch and what happened to Sidney Molson. You might almost call my mother a gift of God, General Kirk.

'Sidney was such a naughty little boy. He was frightened and tried to run away so we had to make an example of him.' Mary glanced from one group of children to the other. Those on the right smiled happily back, but the others stared at her in complete awe like devotees before a priestess.

'None of you will be naughty now, will you, children? You may be frightened, but you will never try to run away. Not after what happened to Sidney Molson. What a weight Sidney was when we carried him out on to the moor; a dead weight.' She giggled and performed another swirling dance, her little feet light on the grass and her gloved arms stretched out towards the fire and the cliff behind it.

'Mary, try and understand what I am going to tell you.' Kirk's mouth felt as if it were choked with cinders and though the fire was scorching his back his teeth were chattering. 'I do not know why you did these things, but I do know that you are not responsible for them. Something has possessed you, my dear, and is controlling you against your own will. Mary Valley didn't torture Sidney Molson, Mary didn't murder those old people on the launch, or burn her own mother alive, but something . . .'

'Didn't Mary Valley kill her mother, General? I thought you saw me cut the ropes.' A child laughed but it sounded like an old woman cackling. 'Anna used to beat me when I was young. She would lock me up in a dark cupboard when her lovers came to visit her. Wicked, wicked Anna Harb, but how loudly she screamed when she felt the fire. Those last few seconds of her life made it all up to me.'

'But the old people in the launch hadn't harmed or beaten you, Mary. They befriended you and looked after you and were always kind to you. Why should you cause their deaths?'

'You still think that?' The rest of the children were laughing now and Mary turned and whispered something to one of the older boys. He nodded and ran off towards the house.

'You have not grasped anything at all, General. You think that some psychic force has possessed us, don't you.' Tears of laughter trickled down the smooth cheeks and dried in the heat of the fire.

'Let me help you to understand, then. Nobody died on that launch. Nobody has been killed except Anna Harb and Haynes and little Sidney Molson. There is nothing evil about the things we have done and all of us are still alive—George L'Eclus, Paul Anderson, Naureen Stokes and the rest of our friends. They are all here with us; secure in our Fellowship of love. The founder is here too, General. That poor clever woman who felt her body melt in a metal box and dreamed a dream of salvation.

'Is it clear to you now, General? Do you realize who we are? Do you still think of me as Mary Harb or Mary Valley?' She pulled off her gloves to show the plump, creamy flesh beneath them.

'No.' Kirk shook his head, seeing the boy returning with a coil of wire slung over his shoulder. Behind his back, the fire crackled, the wind howled and suspicion turned to certainty. An officer of the British army on his knees and in terror before the body of a seven-year-old child.

'Perhaps Anna Harb really did have second sight because she recognized you from the very beginning.' He forced himself to look at the young eyes mocking him and the old evil thing which possessed them. Above the unlined forehead the wind was parting her hair to show a thin white scar and Kirk knew that it was the doorway through which the poison has been inserted.

'You are no longer Mary Harb or Mary Valley. You are "the soul that should not have been born" and your name is Helen Van Traylen.'

Chapter Twenty

'Sir Marcus, this is too much to swallow.' The Chief Constable glowered across the operating theatre. 'You have thrown completely new light on to the case by showing that this man L'Eclus was dead several hours before the launch was sabotaged. I accept your word for that because you are an internationally respected scientist. But what you now suggest is preposterous.' Cameron was longing for a drink and his flask was pressed comfortably against his hip, but the presence of death on the slides and in the metal container held him back.

'You are telling me that L'Eclus and the others may not have been killed at all. That they are still alive.'

'Only part of them will be alive, Chief Constable. I believe that certain areas of their memory centres were removed before death and grafted on to the brains of other human beings.' Marcus's background had made him more cautious than most men. He hated venturing an opinion without definite evidence and he fully sympathized with Cameron's doubts. All the same, his theory was the only one that fitted in with the evidence and he knew it must be correct.

'When my wife telephoned me earlier this evening, she quoted a maxim of Sherlock Holmes which tells one to reject all impossibilities and whatever remains must be the truth, however improbable it appears. Tania and John Forest considered that Mary Valley's dreams were the result of psychic possession. That the child's mind had been taken over by the soul of Mrs Van Traylen. They were wrong about the supernatural and had jumped to a false conclusion due to a lack of sufficient information. The fact that L'Eclus was dead long before the loss of the launch and that all the previous bodies had been mutilated gives us that information and it must add up to the truth, however unpleasant or unlikely it appears.' Marcus kept looking at each of his audience in turn. Cameron and the inspector wore expressions of complete disbelief but Dr Knight was watching him like a terrier at a rat hole.

'It's physically possible, gentlemen, granted a hell of a lot of knowledge, intense research and an insane desire to succeed. Through the work of a number of scientists including those I mentioned, Forbes and Lashley, Ramon Cajal and Laura Tyrell we know a great deal about the nature of memory. By experiments with animals, Lashley discovered that the centres were not localized in a few areas as was once thought, but spread over a wide expanse of the cortex. He also demonstrated that a rat which had been taught certain skills would lose them if the outer layer of its cortex were removed or atrophied.'

'I still do not believe you. Surely it is one thing to destroy cerebral tissue and quite another to transfer it.' Cameron shook his head angrily. Behind him the wind rattled the windows though the room itself was muggy with pipe and cigarette smoke.

'A group of old, frightened people with such a horror of dying that they would attempt to achieve immortality by physically transplanting part of their personalities on to the minds of children. Oh, I know that a lot of progress has been made in cell grafting these days, but it can't be possible. It would go against the whole plan of the creation.' He turned to his enemy, Knight, for support. 'You're a doctor, man. Tell me that Sir Marcus is wrong and it couldn't be done.'

'I am a country G.P., Captain Cameron, nothing more.' Knight added another stub to his already overflowing ashtray. 'But I remember wondering why Laura Tyrell, or Laura Rose as we know her, should bury herself out here to look after a handful of children. She was a very eminent neurologist indeed and her thesis *The Physique of Personality* is still a standard text-book. I can also see where Eric Yeats might fit in. He was one of the fastest surgeons of his day, and speed is essential in all forms of brain surgery because the cells atrophy much faster than any other part of the body. Though I haven't heard the recordings of Mary Valley's night terrors, I am prepared to agree that Sir Marcus may have a case.'

'Thank you, Doctor. Also remember the mutilations.' Marcus gave a slight bow. There was no doubt left in his own mind though the factors of emotion took some understanding. A group of rich and talented people who had been banded together by a common horror of the grave. Had Helen Van Traylen read the same fairy story that had troubled his own childhood? he wondered. The old man toiling up the mountain and the stale, toothless mouth opening to breathe his personality into the body of a child.

But however the idea occurred to her, the woman had grasped it. Was there a chance that the Last Enemy might be conquered? That a portion of the personality, the soul, if one liked the term, could be physically transferred into a strong, new body? If so, there would be no death, no cessation of existence or fear of hell fire, but just a passing from one room into another, as Fawnlee had said. The difficulties must have been enormous and, though the very thought of what Helen Van Traylen had done filled him with nausea, Marcus had to admire her tenacity. First would have come the cautious approaches to discover people with a similar horror of death that overrode all considerations of doubt and morality. The welding of them into a devoted brotherhood and the struggle to keep hope alive during the long years of technical research. Finally the establishment of the orphanage, two bodies, one old and one young, stretched out on the tables and Eric Yeats gowned and ready to perform the first operation.

'Quite so.' Knight had left his chair and was pacing across the room. 'Every one of those people was mutilated after death in one way or another: gravity, a motor vehicle, gunshot, high explosive. They had to be to conceal what had been done to them.' Knight had all the pomposity of the young and he strutted as he spoke.

'As Sir Marcus has pointed out the memory cells are not local-ized in one sector of the brain but distributed over a considerable area. To remove an appreciable portion of them would not only kill the patient but leave a tell-tale scar that would be immediately recognized for what it was.

'The transplantations might be almost unnoticeable however.' He paused, hand on hip, before Cameron and Grant, like a lecturer eying two inattentive students. 'If I were performing such an oper-ation I would drill narrow trephine holes in the skull and insert tubes to freeze and kill a portion of the cortex with liquid nitro-gen. I would then be ready to remove cell tissue in the form of ribonucleic acid from the brain of the donor and introduce it into my patient. The scars would be tiny and soon hidden by a child's hair, but providing the tissues united, the alien memory would be lodged like a parasite, invisible beneath the flesh and bone.'

'All right, Doctor. I will accept that it is physically possible.' Cameron's pipe rapped the wall behind him. 'But I still can't credit it. If you are correct, Sir Marcus, at least ten of those poor little devils must have been infected already. How many so-called deaths have there been to date? Mrs Van Traylen herself, then the old col-onel and the woman novelist and two others, finally half a dozen in the launch and there may be more we don't know about. Now, I suppose fresh children and guardians are being recruited and the whole foul process continues.' The pipe broke against the wall, but he hardly noticed it.

'It is quite unthinkable, Levin. Who would wish to produce such monsters? Children infected and poisoned by the memories of the dead. Creatures with two separate personalities which we cannot recognize. What would one do with such beings? Imprison them? Lock them up in mental homes? Use them as guinea pigs?' He raised the shattered stem of the pipe and pointed it at Marcus.

'No, you must be wrong and, in any case, how does the Harb woman fit in with your theory?'

'I have no idea, Chief Constable.' Marcus had been leaning

against the operating table, but he was suddenly on his feet and staring towards the window and the helicopter parked in the square. He had been concentrating on the technical side of the problem but the mention of Anna Harb made him remember something else.

'Kirk told you that he believed Anna Harb was hiding in the orphanage grounds and the bonfire might bring her out for another attack. He said he intended to go to Inver House himself. If the old boy somehow stumbles on the truth . . .' Marcus pulled the door open and then turned and looked back at them.

'Captain Cameron, Inspector Grant, whether you believe my theory or not, for God's sake let's do something about it.'

Chapter Twenty-one

'YOUR NAME is Helen Van Traylen.' That was the truth at last. The child's head had nodded gaily, she had clapped her hands and giggled at the answer. Then the boy had come running towards her with the wire rope over his shoulder and Kirk saw how he was going to die.

But though his death would be agonizing it was unimportant because he was old and tired and very few people would mourn him. He was quite ready to go home and the only thing that mattered was the sense of utter failure and defeat. There is no fool like an old fool, he thought, standing quite alone facing the flames. They had untied his ankles, but the wire was attached to his wrists and it stretched away from him through the centre of the fire, already reddening in the embers.

When you first saw them you should have recognized them for what they were, he told himself. You should have seen that they were not normal children. You should have recognized the strangeness of them; the aura of evil that came from the twin personalities lodged within a single brain. Because he had been blind, Helen Van Traylen's monstrous scheme would continue unchecked to poison the race.

If only he had been a better actor, he might have succeeded.

The children, he couldn't think of them by another name, had moved off to the other side of the fire, dancing and singing and letting off fireworks and the adults had walked towards him.

They had stood in line before him; Fawnlee and Yeats, Laura Rose and Mrs Alison and the rest of them, and all their faces were full of compassion while one of the women had wept for him.

But they had no guilt at all, not a shred of it. Like the children who had not yet been treated they were completely under the spell of their terrible charges and a compulsive terror of dying had driven them into slavery.

'You are quite correct, General Kirk. Helen and the others are monsters now.' Fawnlee had answered him. 'Their cruelty is that of an unbalanced child who tears the wings from a fly. But they are monsters who are not going to die and once the cells are truly united we believe they will become as normal human beings. In any case Helen is our leader and we can never disobey her.'

Fawnlee was lying. Kirk could see self-deception clear in his face as he described what had been done over the years and the way Helen Van Traylen had bound them together. The sadness and anxiety he had noticed before which had made him think that they realized some dark force was working against them was clear now. These people knew that they had produced a race of degenerates. It saddened them, but had not deterred them. Their terror of the grave, the longing to go on, the shadow of the grey figure of Death waiting at the door was so great that they would accept any escape from it. To them, the Wandering Jew was not a figure of pity but of deep envy.

All the same, in spite of his nausea and the fact that they would allow him to be tortured to death, Kirk had to admire their tenacity. The years of preparation and intense work, the charities built up as fronts, while some of them died and others grew too senile to care and the medical researches produced nothing but records of failure. The personality of Helen Van Traylen had been their motive force, but he wondered who had been the practiced planners. Who, for instance, had driven the Dormobile to the dynamite store and arranged to destroy the launch?

'Yes, General, Mary is a child now, cruel and mentally disturbed, but she will grow into a good human being because her brain houses the soul of a saint.' Laura Rose had pleaded for his understanding and tears had trickled down her worn cheeks.

'When Helen founded our Fellowship she showed us that there was hope. At first she talked to us individually and discovered our longing to go on. She conquered our scruples and proved that there could be a physical resurrection and that life could be bridged from one generation to another.

'God himself gave her that vision, General Kirk. When Helen was trapped in that fire so long ago, he told her that she was his instrument who would bring a great gift to mankind. She passed on her faith to us and supported us in everything. If Eric or I despaired, she encouraged us. When the task appeared impossible, she prayed with us. Then, one day, we saw a sliver of tissue unite with the cortex of an animal and knew that God's promise had been kept.

'Before long it will be my turn, General.' She reached out and touched his hand. 'Whenever one guardian passes over into its secure, new home, another is recruited to take his or her place. Soon Eric and Michael and I will rediscover what it means to run and dance and make love and be young again. To be young, General. To throw away our old, worn-out bodies like discarded clothes and be really young.'

At that moment Kirk destroyed himself. There was a plea and an offer in the woman's eyes and it should have told him what he had to do. He should have confessed to a similar horror of dying and congratulated them and begged to join with them. But the things he had seen had driven out reason and anger was like the glare of the fire and the crackling heat of the blazing timbers and the steady wind blowing in over the cliffs.

'You are lying to yourself, Dr Rose,' he said. 'You will never be young again. All you can do is to graft part of your old, diseased personality into the body of a child and produce a monster that will rot in an asylum.' The words came gasping out through his dry lips and he looked at the group of uninfected children, abject and cowed near the edge of the cliff.

'You spoke of God just now, madam, but you are fighting

against his whole intention. You would put your fears, your memories, your old woman's sickness into the soul of a little girl. Don't
you realize that that is the sin which will never be forgiven you?
You may let your mutants drag me into that fire, Dr Rose, but it
will be nothing to the fire that burns you one day.'

They left him then. One by one, the old people filed away back
across the field and the creatures they had made returned to him.

'You have refused Laura's offer, General.' Mary Valley, Kirk still
tried to think of her by that name, smiled up at him. 'You will not
accept the gift of life which God gave me to pass on to others.'

'Mary, it was not God. Part of you is still a normal child, Mary,
so try and understand. Fight the wickedness, the memories of
that woman which have been grafted on to your mind. God didn't
make you do those things. Would God have made you torture
your mother and Sidney Molson? Remember the way Sidney died,
Mary; the wounds on his hands and feet and the cuts on his forehead. God didn't tell you to do that.'

'Didn't he?' For an instant there was a puzzled look on her face,
but it cleared instantly. 'My God ordered it, whatever his name
may be, General.' The child tittered, an old woman cackled and
a thing grinned at him. A creature which would remain split and
diseased till the end of its life.

If life ever did end, that was. When the creatures became old
would more young victims be found to act as hosts to them? Could
the process be repeated over and over again till the whole race
became tainted and a great army of the damned populated the
earth?

'What's in a name, General Kirk? Whatever my God is called
he has proved his powers.' The slight body jumped up and down
in triumph. 'Our God has given us life and what can yours do?
That driver who refused to stop smoking when I told him to had
a god. "Christ, Jesus Christ", he kept repeating when the cigarette
burned his face and the coach went out of control.' The smile vanished and a sour, bitter frown puckered the smooth features.

'And like the driver you have refused to obey me. Get ready, my
friends. Let's have a tug of war and see if General Kirk has a god
as strong as ours.' The rest of the mutants ran off to the other side

of the fire and Kirk felt the wire tighten. 'Pull, children, Billy, Jane, Malcolm, pull hard and we will sing as he screams to his god.' She capered at the edge of the flames and the wire started to drag him forward.

'They will discover who you are, Helen Van Traylen.' There was no escape, no appeal, no hope. His ashes would be scattered or buried and nobody would ever suspect what had happened to him. Death was a few yards away, already he could feel his skin cracking in the heat, but it was unimportant. All that mattered was the knowledge that he had failed and those poor, split, but intensely evil creatures would go undetected.

'They will lock you away in asylums and study you like infected guinea pigs. Men like Marcus Levin will write theses about you and journalists will have a field day. I can think of a good title for them. "The Monsters of Bala".' Kirk's only consolation was that he might inflict some slight mental pain before he died.

'Nobody will find us. Nobody will ever lock us up. That was promised to me as well.' Above the roar of the flames, he heard an old voice crack with fury. The voice of a woman who had cowered in a steel box and felt her body start to shrivel. Was that the thing that had started her mania? he wondered. A vision of hell fire that sent her striving for immortality. Even as the rope dragged his own body forward, Kirk felt a slight twinge of compassion.

'Go on, pull, my friends.' Round and round she danced beside him, the long dress blowing in the wind and the fair hair streaming to reveal the tiny scars through which the poison had been inserted. 'Pull hard and sing.'

Kirk's feet clawed at the earth, he tried to brace himself against tussocks of grass, but the wire moved, the earth slid by and the things beyond the fire sang. Through the crackle of blazing timber he could hear their voices, shrill and birdlike. 'Here we come gathering nuts in May, nuts in May, nuts in May.' Inch by inch, foot by foot, he was dragged towards his death while the figure of a blonde child capered and sang at his side. 'Here we come gathering nuts in May on a cold and frosty morning.'

The pain was agonizing now and the wind appeared to be much stronger, driving the flames straight towards him like rapiers to pierce his eyes. It felt as if his whole body was melting, but he wouldn't scream and he wouldn't cry out. No, he must not give them that satisfaction. He closed his eyes, and all at once faces from both the past and the future were before him. His wife and his daughter, Alan smiling from under a blue midshipman's cap as if welcoming him home, his parents, Tania and Marcus and the imagined face of their child he would never see. Beyond them, faceless and in shadow, but kinder, gentler, more loving and merciful than anything he had ever known, stood the Last Enemy and he pitied those who resisted him.

'Help me to fight to the end. Don't let me cry out or make a sound. They mustn't hear me so much as whimper.' The faces were obscured by flame and smoke and Kirk prayed to his God that he might die with dignity. He threw himself down on to the scorched earth, clutching at grass and heather, but the wire still forced him forward, while suddenly above the sounds of the fire and the wind and the singing voices there was a great hammering, pulsing roar which he knew must come from his own imagination. He realized he was about to faint and had been given the grace to go out in silence and he raised his head to take one final look at the world he was leaving. As he did so, the hammering sound lessened and he did cry out, but not in pain or despair. The wire had gone slack and it was Mary Valley . . . Helen Van Traylen who screamed because the wind had veered to the north and she herself was burning.

A shower of sparks had caught her dress and set it alight in a dozen places. With her mouth open in a constant cracked scream she beat at them and staggered back, and out from the bonfire came a great gout of flame which wrapped her like a robe. Her companions rushed to her aid but the flame held them back as it stripped the hair from her head and the clothes from her body and, all at once, it wasn't a child's body any more. Kirk saw an old, stunted woman totter towards the edge of the cliff and heard an immensely old voice croak while a crone's eyes glared at him.

'I curse your god, General Kirk. I curse everything which is cruel and mean.' Her hands tore at the red searing blanket that wrapped her, but the wind still blew, the flames roared and her feet stumbled on towards the abyss. 'Why should he have given us a vision of eternity and then left me alone in the dark?'

For perhaps five seconds, but they seemed like hours, Kirk watched her hover between rock and air and then there was suddenly no more pain, no light, no sensation or thought for him; only the void; nothing at all.

Chapter Twenty-two

'CHARLES, it is all right. Everything is going to be quite all right.' The voice sounded as if it came from a great distance and he appeared to be wearing spectacles with bright yellow frames. Through them Kirk saw Marcus Levin's face beaming down at him. 'Very soon we are going to put you to sleep again, but first I want you to know that you are out of danger and there will be no permanent disfigurement.'

'Thank you, Mark. I expect I shall be a nasty sight for some time, but not to worry. I never was much of an oil painting.' Kirk tried to smile through the slits in the tannin-soaked bandages, but his lips and eyelids would not obey him. He could remember the agony as he had been hauled towards the fire, how his whole body felt as if it were melting, the faces he had seen and how the wind had suddenly changed and the wire had gone slack. But, beyond that, he could remember nothing at all.

'I wanted to die, Mark. I honestly believe that I saw Death and I wanted to go to him.'

'Sorry you were disappointed, Charles, but you've got a constitution like a horse.' Marcus was kneeling beside his stretcher. 'You'll just have to carry on being a senile delinquent for a few more years, I'm afraid.'

'I suppose so.' Once again Kirk tried to form his cracked lips into a smile, but it was quite useless. 'How long have I been unconscious, dear boy?'

'About an hour and you're very weak and full of dope, so try not to talk.' Behind Marcus, the fire had dwindled to a mere heap of smoking embers and the clouds had blown away, leaving a clear sky and a big white moon to light up the hills.

'In a moment, we're going to put you out again and take you to hospital. But before they move you I want you to understand that it is all over and there is no need to worry about anything.'

'Yes, it is over. Dead and done with.' Kirk moved his face towards the edge of the cliff and everything came back to him. The scream, the curses and the little figure in its cloak of flame staggering out into the darkness. Beyond the cliff he could make out a line of silver which was the sands of Spaniards' Bay. ' "God blew with his wind and they were broken", Mark.'

'I'm not with you, Charles. What has the Armada inscription got to do with it?' Marcus frowned and then his face cleared and he pointed towards the R.A.F. helicopter drawn up beside an ambulance and two police cars.

'No, it wasn't God, I'm afraid. That was the thing which blew. I commandeered it at Lochern and when the pilot saw what they were doing to you, he brought her in close. The rotors fanned the flames towards that . . . that child, woman, thing, whatever you like to call her and she ran back over the cliff. My dear, clever wife is the one we have to thank God for. Tania telephoned me from London and gave a theory which helped us to put two and two together.'

'Don't let them take me yet, Mark.' Two ambulance men were waiting to lift the stretcher, but Kirk waved them aside. He had to hear the end of the story in the place where it had actually happened. 'You know everything, Mark? What they were . . . what they had become . . . what was done to them?'

'Almost everything, Charles. While you were unconscious Cameron and Inspector Grant had a nice cosy chat with Fawnlee and the others and I gather they have told the truth.

'But what will they do to him and his companions, that's what I want to know? What possible punishment can there be? Children, little children.' Marcus's face was flushed with anger. 'The rest of the kids are all right, that's the only mercy. But the others . . . !'

'Kids . . . Children.' Kirk shook his head. 'You call them that because you don't understand anything, Mark. You don't realize who they are even now. Those creatures weren't children any more. They were . . .'

'Take it easy please, General Kirk.' Dr Knight was at the other side of the stretcher and he reached for his pulse. 'Sir Marcus was referring to the children who had not been treated yet. They ran away when the helicopter landed but they have all been rounded up and are safe and sound. The others are dead. They went like the rats of Norway.'

'Norway rats? You mean lemmings?' Kirk closed his eyes for a moment. He was so weak that it was an effort to concentrate on anything. Lemmings; the rats of Norway. Small rodents with suicidal tendencies which every three years join in a mass migration, ravaging the crops in a straight line till they reach the cliffs and the beaches and go on to meet certain death in the sea.

'That's right, Charles, they followed her.' Marcus nodded towards the cliff. 'I saw it happen and we don't have to worry about them. When their leader fell, they went after her. One and all, they threw themselves over the edge as though they had been tied to her by strings.

'Strange, isn't it? Those people longed for actual, physical immortality. They feared death so much that they would go to any lengths to avoid it and, in a sense, they succeeded. Yet, when they saw their leader die, they followed her. In a fiendish way, theirs really was a fellowship.'

'You could call it that.' The embers were dying, caving in, subsiding and Kirk looked away. Somewhere among the glow were the remains of the woman they had hunted with troops and dogs and machines; the one they had judged guilty of everything while, all the time, the real demons had walked secure and unafraid to propagate a race which was as maimed and crippled as his own torn hand. Without a hunch, an accident and Tania Levin, they might have gone undetected for generations. In his mind's eye, Kirk could picture the successors of Eric Yeats and Laura Rose squinting down at another drugged little body and preparing to graft a sliver of old decayed tissue on to the brain of a child.

'But you are sure they are dead; all of them?' The very thought of one creature remaining alive sickened him and Kirk croaked the question. 'You are quite certain . . . All?'

'There is no doubt about that. The cliff is a hundred and fifty feet high and they have been dashed to pieces on the rocks or swept out to sea long ago.' Something glinted in Marcus's hand. 'There'll be no frightened, split children to rot in asylums. Nothing to worry about.

'Now, you're going to have a good long rest and wake up in hospital, beddy-byes for you, Charles.' Kirk felt a prick in his arm and the ambulance men stooped forward to raise the stretcher.

The moon was high above the island now, and as they carried him away Kirk saw a long stream of golden light creeping across the bay. It was very beautiful, but he was glad to feel the injection start to work. The bodies beneath the cliff belonged to monsters, but they had been children once and that strip of gleaming, heaving water reminded him of a child's flowing hair.

NEW & FORTHCOMING TITLES FROM VALANCOURT BOOKS

R. C. Ashby (Ruby Ferguson)	He Arrived at Dusk
Frank Baker	The Birds
Walter Baxter	Look Down in Mercy
Charles Beaumont	The Hunger and Other Stories
David Benedictus	The Fourth of June
John Blackburn	A Scent of New-Mown Hay
	Broken Boy
	Blue Octavo
	The Flame and the Wind
	Nothing But the Night
	Bury Him Darkly
	The Household Traitors
	Our Lady of Pain
	The Face of the Lion
	The Cyclops Goblet
	A Beastly Business
Thomas Blackburn	The Feast of the Wolf
John Braine	Room at the Top
	The Vodi
Basil Copper	The Great White Space
	Necropolis
Hunter Davies	Body Charge
Jennifer Dawson	The Ha-Ha
Ronald Fraser	Flower Phantoms
Stephen Gilbert	The Burnaby Experiments
Martyn Goff	The Plaster Fabric
	The Youngest Director
Stephen Gregory	The Cormorant
Claude Houghton	I Am Jonathan Scrivener
	This Was Ivor Trent
Gerald Kersh	Nightshade and Damnations
Francis King	To the Dark Tower
	Never Again
	An Air that Kills
	The Dividing Stream
	The Dark Glasses
	The Man on the Rock
C.H.B. Kitchin	Ten Pollitt Place
	The Book of Life

HILDA LEWIS	The Witch and the Priest
KENNETH MARTIN	Aubade
	Waiting for the Sky to Fall
MICHAEL McDOWELL	The Amulet
MICHAEL NELSON	Knock or Ring
	A Room in Chelsea Square
BEVERLEY NICHOLS	Crazy Pavements
OLIVER ONIONS	The Hand of Kornelius Voyt
DENNIS PARRY	Sea of Glass
ROBERT PHELPS	Heroes and Orators
J.B. PRIESTLEY	Benighted
	The Other Place
FORREST REID	The Garden God
	The Tom Barber Trilogy
	At the Door of the Gate
	The Spring Song
HENRY DE VERE STACPOOLE	The Blue Lagoon
RUSSELL THORNDIKE	The Slype
	The Master of the Macabre
JOHN TREVENA	Furze the Cruel
	Sleeping Waters
JOHN WAIN	Hurry on Down
	The Smaller Sky
HUGH WALPOLE	The Killer and the Slain
KEITH WATERHOUSE	There is a Happy Land
	Billy Liar
ALEC WAUGH	The Loom of Youth
COLIN WILSON	Ritual in the Dark
	Man Without a Shadow
	The World of Violence
	The Philosopher's Stone
	The God of the Labyrinth

Selected Eighteenth and Nineteenth Century Classics

ANONYMOUS	Teleny
	The Sins of the Cities of the Plain
GRANT ALLEN	Miss Cayley's Adventures
JOANNA BAILLIE	Six Gothic Dramas
EATON STANNARD BARRETT	The Heroine
WILLIAM BECKFORD	Azemia
MARY ELIZABETH BRADDON	Thou Art the Man

JOHN BUCHAN	Sir Quixote of the Moors
HALL CAINE	The Manxman
MONA CAIRD	The Wing of Azrael
MARIE CORELLI	The Sorrows of Satan
	Ziska
CAROLINE CLIVE	Paul Ferroll
BARON CORVO	Stories Toto Told Me
	Hubert's Arthur
GABRIELE D'ANNUNZIO	The Intruder (L'innocente)
JOHN DAVIDSON	Earl Lavender
THOMAS DE QUINCEY	Klosterheim
ARTHUR CONAN DOYLE	The Parasite
	Round the Red Lamp
BARON DE LA MOTTE FOUQUÉ	The Magic Ring
H. RIDER HAGGARD	Nada the Lily
ERNEST G. HENHAM	Tenebrae
CHARLES JOHNSTONE	Chrysal (2 vols)
CAROLINE LAMB	Glenarvon
FRANCIS LATHOM	The Midnight Bell
SOPHIA LEE	The Two Emilys
SHERIDAN LE FANU	Carmilla
	The Cock and Anchor
	The Rose and the Key
M. G. LEWIS	The Monk
EDWARD BULWER LYTTON	Eugene Aram
FLORENCE MARRYAT	The Blood of the Vampire
RICHARD MARSH	The Beetle
	The Goddess: A Demon
	The Complete Sam Briggs Stories
BERTRAM MITFORD	Renshaw Fanning's Quest
	The Sign of the Spider
	The Weird of Deadly Hollow
JOHN MOORE	Zeluco
OUIDA	Under Two Flags
	In Maremma
ELIZA PARSONS	Castle of Wolfenbach
	The Mysterious Warning
WALTER PATER	Marius the Epicurean
ROSA PRAED	Fugitive Anne
BRAM STOKER	The Lady of the Shroud
	The Mystery of the Sea

CPSIA information can be obtained at www.ICGtesting.com
Printed in the USA
LVOW131352120413

328878LV00003B/500/P